The Scent of Dreams

The Dream Factory, Book #4

Shéa MacLeod and Linda Mercury

Mercury/MacLeod Press

Chapter One

Beauty is not about what is on the outside. It is about what makes you feel magnificent.

How to Take Over the World: Affirmations for Glorious Femmes

Sophia de Luca wanted two things in life. She wanted to bring people joy and she wanted to forget that Emelio Greco ever existed, let alone broke her heart.

And heavens, she was in the middle of an amazing start. Gold Coast's tiny fashion show, "Little Milan: Bringing the Classics Home," would start in a few hours. Despite her jet lag, she'd never had as much fun before. Inside the barber shop, she and an older man smoothed the children's hair into ponytails and slicked-back Italian styles. The barber had nodded at her, his face a study of suspicion, but he showed the boys how to use gel and pomade to achieve the necessary sophisticated styles. All the young people giggled, even the manliest of boys, as she dusted a little powder over their noses and introduced the joys of petroleum jelly to make their lips look moisturized. Using disposable spoolie brushes, she showed the interested ones how jelly could darken their lashes and make them stand out.

Cassia Mack, her dear friend, came to her in a lull, dragging a tired-looking woman behind her. Sophia raised her eyebrows as the duo approached. Obviously, this was Cassia's mother. They shared the strong bone structure and eye color. Alice Kennedy, the show's organizer, followed a few steps behind.

"Sophia, this is my mother, Joan Mark. Mom, this is Sophia de Luca."

Alice took over. "I want Joan to be the show topper. Here's the dress." She brandished a black satin dress, cocktail-length, but with a tulle floor-length bustle. "What can you do?"

Sophia gave Joan a long once over, letting her experienced stylist's eye take in every detail. She'd had to rush with the young people, doing quick pick-me-ups. For a grand finale, she'd need a more complete look. Joan shifted in discomfort at the frank gaze, obviously convinced she would not measure up.

Sophia imagined that for most of her life, Joan hadn't measured up, certainly not within herself. Everything about her, from the bowed line of her neck to her hunched shoulders, screamed of someone who was trying to become invisible.

Sophia did not do invisible.

In her current brown shirt and overalls, Joan looked pallid, slouchy, and washed out. With the dramatic black dress, she would need some color, some excitement, something to make her stand up, stand out. The look came immediately to Sophia's mind, faster than ever.

"I know exactly what she needs," Sophia breathed to Alice and Cassia. "Mrs. Mark, please take a seat."

Joan chewed on her lips but sat in the hairstyling chair. "Just call me Joan."

It came out as a low mutter Sophia barely caught, but she did, and it brought a smile to her face. Progress!

"Joan, then. Now. Be prepared to meet your true self." Sophia flipped a towel over Joan's chest. "I don't have time to do what I want, so we will improvise." Sophia stroked Joan's shoulders, which vibrated with tension. She reminded Sophia a little of Cassie when they first met in Rome. If anyone needed a little magic, it was Joan. "A quick twist, some brown glitter spray, it will work."

Joan frowned. Heavy grooves appeared on either side of her mouth. "I'm just an old farm wife. I am not pretty."

"Pretty." Sophia snorted. "You will not be pretty. You will be magnificent!" Moving rapidly, she twisted Joan's dry, rough hair into a sophisticated, minimalistic bun. She grabbed the can of brown glitter and used it to temporarily dye Joan's hair a sleek, mink-brown color. She stood back and studied the reflection in the mirror. "Good start. What do you think?"

"I've always worn bangs," Joan stuttered, eyes wide.

"Not anymore," Sophia returned, already looking through the make-up kit the drama teacher had loaned her. "Aha." She held up a fluffy brush loaded with a light golden powder. "This. We will use this."

Joan's skin needed work, but for a fast foundation, the slight glimmer would give her color. Sophia stroked the brush gently across Joan's cheekbones and along her forehead and jawline. Yes, this would work very well.

Joan closed her eyes at the sensation of brushes on her skin. "That feels good," she murmured.

"You deserve to feel good, Joan," Sophia replied, darkening the arch of her subject's brows. Next up, some stylish black eyeliner to give Joan the necessary dramatic eyes this dress demanded.

"If you say so."

Sophia smirked. "I do say so." She was never wrong about beauty and glamor, at least. Other things... Well, that was best left alone.

Next, she selected a classic matte bright red lipstick. Joan had good lips, full but pale. Time to change that. With a thin brush, she filled the color from upper to lower. A touch of the petroleum jelly in the center of her lower lip created a more sensual look.

Sophia stood in front of the mirror, blocking the view. "Now, go put on that dress," she ordered Joan.

"Can't I see?" she pouted.

"Not yet. You must see the whole effect." Sophia smiled. "Go, go!"

Joan scurried behind the dressing screen. Moments later, she emerged, no longer a shaggy, timid caterpillar, but a magnificent, dramatic moth. The black dress hugged her body, showing off every dramatic curve. Her pale skin glowed against the dark, smooth fabric.

"Now." Sophia stepped aside, letting Joan look.

"Oh, my God." Joan Mark clasped her hands over her mouth and burst into tears. "I can't believe it," she sobbed.

"No, no," Sophia dabbed at Joan's face with a makeup sponge. "You must not ruin your makeup. Save the tears for later." Thank heavens she had used the petroleum jelly.

Joan held it together but wheezed for a second. "I didn't know," she whispered. "I didn't know I was..."

"Beautiful. Yes." Sophia nodded firmly at Joan's headshake. "You are beautiful and now you know it. In fact..." She snapped a quick picture and sent it to Cassia. "Now, your daughter will not let you forget. And if you do, she will remind you."

Alice walked by with her tablet. She glanced at Joan and stopped dead. "Yes, yes, yes," she gasped. "This! This is what I wanted for my dress. Joan, you look...incredible. Sophia, you are a genius. We will bring the house down."

Joan beamed. Sophia smiled back at her.

Alice dashed over to the curtain and called, "Places everyone."

Sophia's phone buzzed in her pocket. Since she had a moment before she had to get into her own outfit, she checked it.

Emelio stopped by the bakery just now. He asked us where you were. We said we don't know. Just wanted to give you a heads up in case he tries to reach you. Love you, Mom.

Sophia snorted. Where did that boy get his nerve? He dumped her. And now he seemed to think it was his business to know where she was and who she was with? Absolutely not! She certainly hadn't told him her plans to travel.

I won't give him the time of day. She texted back. *Besides, look at this.* She sent her the picture of Joan. *This is what I have done today.*

So beautiful! Her mother's text came back. *You, my darling Sophia, are pure magic.*

Love you, Mama.

Hidden behind the big canvas tent, the children lined up for their turn on the catwalk. Everyone's posture straightened as Dr. Merv opened the show. His cheerful voice boomed out, welcoming one and all to Gold Coast.

Sophia's phone buzzed again. She saw Emelio's number on the screen. She shoved the phone back into her pocket and got ready for her entrance. To the devil with him. She had a job to do now.

When Joan finally took the stage in her red opera gloves and her black satin slip with the faux bustle on the back, Gold

Coast erupted in cheers. Two teenaged girls in the front burst into tears. Sophia clasped her hands to her heart. Fashion and hair might seem frivolous to some people, but she knew they were the gateway to creating your ideal world.

Chapter Two

Your hidden talents need to see the light.

How to Take Over the World: Affirmations for Glorious Femmes

E melio Greco never wanted to cook another meal in his life.

He sat on a bench by the Colosseum, idly re-reading one of the historical plaques for what must have been the millionth time. Early every morning, he would sneak out of his home and drink his cappuccino near some ancient monument before the tourists would show up. It was the only quiet time he ever got.

The bitter coffee and frothed milk fortified him for another round of thinking about his life. He'd started with peeling potatoes in his parents' kitchen at age seven and now he resented food. Cooking had become a blur to him, one long memory of aching legs, burns, cuts, exhaustion, and being yelled at. Sophia's ideas had saved his family's struggling restaurant, but she had mostly saved him from his parents' unending criticism.

"*You will never be able to grill octopus correctly,*" his father had said when Emelio was twelve. "*I don't even know why I bother teaching you. You will be the ruin of this family's legacy.*"

The first time he cooked for her, Sophia had said, "*You have an amazing touch with octopus. The seasoning is perfect.*"

At fifteen, his mother held his chin, looked into his face, and said, "*At least you are pretty, even if you can't cook. You will have to find a wife before you lose your looks. She must cook, Emelio. Otherwise, we are doomed.*" Italian mothers were supposed to love and spoil their sons, he thought grimly, licking some of the milk off his upper lip.

The memories were more bitter than his espresso drink. He set down the cup and pulled a sketchbook from his messenger bag. He picked up a thin piece of charcoal. Carefully, he took off his jacket, rolled up his white shirt sleeves, and started sketching the bricks of the ancient amphitheater. As his hand moved over the paper, his brain kept going. Sophia had said so many nice things to him about his cooking and his fashion sense.

With a deft hand, he filled in the paper with shade and light.

He gritted his teeth. He had tried to show his art to his family but that went about as well as anything else he had done. No one, not even his many aunts and uncles, understood his vision of how Italian men should dress. Certainly, they needed to resist the ugly shorts and sloppy shirts that were slowly infiltrating the population.

His father refused to understand that Emelio's passion didn't lie in cuisine. He didn't mind smaller projects, but production cooking exhausted him. They were always trying to force him to be something he was not and making him feel stupid for it.

He hadn't shown Sophia his sketchbook, though. That was too much vulnerability for him. He curved the charcoal around, sketching in a man. Here was his true love, he mused, filling in the details of the Neapolitan semi-structured suit jacket. The British could keep their armor-like suits with structure and bravado. Let the Milanese keep their completely loose jackets. He felt that the Naples-style suit with the relaxed shoulders and rolled lapels truly enhanced masculinity and the studied carelessness of sprezzatura, that unique, graceful effortlessness of style.

He smiled at the drawing. There. That summed up his vision of the perfect Italian man: sharp dressed, but ready for any kind of activity.

Unfortunately, his time was done, and he had to return to the Greco family restaurant. The corners of his mouth turned down again and he dragged his feet over the cobblestones.

As for the rest of his family, at least his younger sister kept her mouth shut. She had gotten the cooking gene. In fact, her food was some of the best around, but Papa limited her in the restaurant kitchen. She wasn't allowed to change the menu despite her talents. Their parents insisted that he do it even though he wasn't nearly as creative.

He never could figure out why his parents did that.

Sophia had never made him feel stupid. She used to look at him like he was a genius. She enjoyed his company and would brainstorm recipes with him. Her creative mind lifted him to new heights. If he were completely honest, it was her ideas that had brought success back to the restaurant, although of course he took credit. There was no sense giving his parents more ammunition against him and there was little else he could take credit for.

But then she bored him when she started talking about her own career. Sophia's job took her attention away from him. He hadn't liked it. In fact, he hated how glowing she got when she talked about uplifting women, how her thought experiments about perfume engaged her mind, how she was able to express herself with fashion and art.

Resentment thinned his mouth. He should be the one who was successful with art. He was the artist, after all.

With her distracted by her business, he got restless. He didn't like being reminded of her success and his lack. He wanted new adventures. He wanted to try things with new women. If one woman could make him a success, three or four or five would certainly do even more for him. Imagine all the support they would give him. The ideas! He would be able to retire from the heat and noise and chaos of the kitchen to a comfortable chair in an office, tasting wine and giving interviews. He was already popular in the Italian press. He would be an international star in no time!

Breaking up with her had seemed the best choice. He didn't need her anymore and there were plenty of others who would happily take her place, pay him the attention he craved, and support his dreams without being distracted by nonsense.

After all, she had written the copy for their website, gotten him in touch with the press. She had nothing else to give him.

He walked through the kitchen door where his sister chopped huge sprigs of rosemary, the aroma more potent than the coffee he had drunk. She glanced up and pursed her lips before returning her attention to her knife work. The funny thing about Guilia was she never resented or blamed him for the fact their parents wouldn't let her have free rein in the kitchen. Instead, she did her best to protect him even though he was the older of the two.

"Papa is upset," she warned him. "There have been fewer tables filled in the last week."

"He was upset when we were booked solid," he groused back, rolling up his sleeves and washing his hands. Did nothing make this family happy?

"I know," she said softly, scraping the chopped sage into a bowl. "Just...be prepared."

Bitterness rose like bile in his throat, threatening to choke him. Why was life so unfair? Why couldn't he have what he wanted?

Chapter Three

Forgive your quirks and embrace your individuality.

How to Take Over the World: Affirmations for Glorious Femmes

L ate that night, after Cassia fell asleep in the shared bed in the apartment above the bakery, Sophia twisted the taps on the bath and let the tub fill. The steam from the hot water flirted with the Art Nouveau, Egyptian-styled furnishings, like the painted lotus flowers on the walls. Tonight, with the fashion show, she had made a giant first step toward making her dreams come true. She'd not once thought of Emelio, and she'd already made a difference at Gold Coast, Illinois. Such a sweet success.

The look on Joan's face when she'd first seen herself in the mirror? Priceless. Sophia wanted to make more people feel that way.

She needed to celebrate such an amazing beginning to her adventure. Taking the box of sea salt from the kitchen, she dumped a cup into the water along with a little baking soda. A final spritz of her favorite perfume over the top of the tub and behold. Her own personal spa.

The soft light of candles filled the room. What a luxury.

She'd never seen such a large bathroom before. And the silence! Rome truly never slept. Back home, her family was always laughing and calling to each other, in addition to the street noise of Vespas and tourists. All through the night came the sounds of rumbling motors and drunken celebrations as people staggered home from the bars. She'd once heard a woman complain that she couldn't open her windows at night for the noise. It had never bothered Sophia much. After all, she'd been born in Rome. Lived her whole life there. The noise pollution was a background soundtrack to her life. But she found she enjoyed the quiet here more than she thought she would.

It was true, everything in the United States was bigger, even in this tiny town. Gold Coast was a far cry from her beloved city. There, she could wander for years and never see everything. Here, she could walk down Main Street from the barber shop to an unusual place named Books and Bait—she had no idea what sort of shop *that* was, but she was dying to find out—in under fifteen minutes. This place completely threw off her sense of scale.

It was disconcerting, but also very freeing.

She tipped her head back against the edge of the bathtub and read the words the long-ago proprietress of the bakery had painted on the ceiling.

Baths are where women dream.

Then thoughts of Emelio weaseled into her brain like the creep he was. He'd been so exciting when they met, showing her what it meant to be young. Her parents usually took her to museums and libraries that showcased history and the past.

Emelio, though, showed Sophia excitement. No longer was she home at night, every night, drinking warm milk with her parents. Instead, she got to see hot new bands, go shopping at the beautiful boutiques, laugh with other people her age, and dance until her feet hurt. Rome wasn't all ancient buildings. It was a vibrant metropolis with some of the best things life had to offer.

Emelio had showed her that.

She sighed. Fine. In the tub was the best place to see what it was he wanted. She lifted her phone and squinted at the text he'd sent.

Where are you? I need all the receipts you have for the purchases you made. I want to get reimbursed for that money.

He wanted to be paid for the things she had bought? Could he be more disgusting? Her stomach flipped over in revulsion. First, she had bought those games and made those coloring books, not him. Now he wanted her to give that money up? How could he ask this? Had he always been this self-absorbed?

Before the breakup, she and Emelio had planned their own food and beauty dominion in Rome. Between his family's restaurant and her family's famous bakery, Dolci di Paradisio, they would shoot to the top of the Roman culinary scene. With her marketing experience and his recipes, they would make an empire of feeling good.

As a stylist, she loved supporting people in making their dreams come true. She had loved brainstorming with Emelio to make his food dreams a reality. But once she had started plugging her business, he had lost interest.

Then came the very bad day.

"I'll go look for some retro games," she told him over their after-dinner Sambuca alla mosca. *"The restaurant is getting*

more popular, and many people are waiting too long. This will keep them happy and amused while they see other people eat."

"Yes, get right on that." He chewed on the coffee beans in the Sambuca. "I want to see other people, by the way."

"I'll go look in some of the secondhand stores...." She stared at him. "What?"

"I want an open relationship." He sat back and crossed his arms like he did when he thought she wasn't following his thoughts fast enough. Like she was stupid. "An. Open. Relationship." He enunciated every syllable.

Her lungs seized up. They had just made wonderful love the night before, passionate and sweaty. She scrambled to make sense of the whole thing. She knew that people had such relationships, but that had never been something she wanted for herself. That had never even been discussed. In fact, he'd always been quite clear that they should be monogamous.

"Do you have a crush on someone?" she'd asked.

He'd laughed at her back then and told her not to be ridiculous. That crushes were for children, though she noticed he never answered her question.

That night and every single one after, he whined and bullied and told her that him being away from her on a date was the same as if he was away at work, so why was she making such a big deal of it? Wasn't she a modern woman?

While she knew several people who enjoyed such relationships, Sophia simply wasn't wired that way. She offered solutions: more sexy play, more time alone with each other without work. He wouldn't budge.

She even asked—although not seriously—if he would be fine with *her* seeing other people in this "open relationship." Big surprise, he threw a fit. Not so open then. He wanted to roam but he wanted her to only see him. She was definitely not okay with that.

A month later, he walked out, leaving her feeling like her stomach had been ripped from her body. For days, she cried in her bedroom, trying to muffle her sobs so she wouldn't disturb her parents.

After the breakup, Emelio started talking smack about her family's business in the local press.

"Here at Greco's, we are the future of Roman dining. The old style is dying. People don't want the same old baked goods anymore or anyone trying to reclaim their past days of glory."

"Are you referring to Il Dolci del Paradisio?" *the reporter had asked.*

"I refuse to name names," he said, waving a hand. "But if you know, you know."

A little voice inside of her said yes, he had always been more into what she could do for him. She had gotten very good at ignoring that little voice during her time with Emelio. But what if she listened to it now?

For curiosity's sake, she checked his social media.

It was a video of him doing a tour of his family's restaurant, complete with a whole lot of, "Look what I did," and people lined up, playing the vintage games she had bought for him.

She slid deeper into the hot water and let it draw out her sadness. She wrung out the washcloth and placed it over her eyes as if she could block out the images of his derision. No, she would not go down this road again.

Fortunately, her new friend, Cassia Mack, had swooped in and helped the de Lucas revitalize their bakery. She had followed Cassia back to this village to help with this brilliant local fashion show.

She plunged her hands deep into the hot water and splashed it on her chest.

No ideas on how to restore her heart from Emelio. For now, she would focus on bringing joy to people here. Perhaps in helping others find their joy, she would find hers.

She just wanted to know why she couldn't stop thinking about him. If she couldn't figure it out, she'd surely do something dramatic and over the top.

That night, Sophia slept fitfully. Early in the morning, she tiptoed through the apartment, carrying her shoes in her hand. Rather than disturb Cassia while she prepped the bakery, Sophia had decided to go outdoors and stretch her legs. She couldn't think of what else to do besides spend more time on social media, looking at Emelio's posts. Every word she read was like being stabbed by thorns, but she couldn't stop.

As she passed through the small living area, a book fell off the shelf and onto the floor in front of her, flipped open to a page with a beautiful botanical drawing of flowers. She read the text:

Your destiny is closer than you think.

What a wonderful thought. Tucking the book under her arm, she wandered from the bakery's front door around to the Betsy Whitaker Memorial Rose Garden. The sun was rising, banishing the gloom of the night. The roses emerged from the light, delicate drops of dew trembling on the petals. She yawned, letting the flowers soothe her nervous system. A splash of golden yellow caught her attention. She knelt before a bush that was heavy with lush blooms. She cupped her hands around a rose, letting the warmth from her palms stimulate the flower's volatile oils. Slowly, the aroma opened up, the sweet and pepper scent reaching her nose.

"Ah," she sighed. Scent was a touchstone for her. She loved how it could excite or calm, create memories, or lift the spirits. Combining this love with style, design, and beauty, she could bring pep and self-care to this farming town.

During the fashion show, she had noticed that the people here had dull, sun-damaged skin, and many of the younger ones had acne problems. She knew how to help with these health concerns.

An older woman, wearing a faded orange head-wrap and torn overalls, ambled through the garden, snipping off fading blossoms and putting them in a long rectangular basket. "Oh, hello," she said when she met Sophia's gaze. "I'm Blanche Sandersen." She smoothed her wrap and held out a hand. "Are you Cassie's friend from Rome?"

Sophia automatically noticed the woman's sunburn and the split ends escaping the wrap as they shook hands. But with a little magic and sunscreen, yes, Blanche could look radiant, like a Roman goddess in draped clothing and curls over her brow. "Yes. I am Sophia de Luca."

"The fashion show was wonderful, wasn't it?" After their handshake, Blanche fiddled with the collar of her shirt, covering the notch at the base of her throat.

"Alice is very talented," Sophia returned. Was Blanche always this nervous? She glanced down at the full basket of wilted yet still sweet-smelling flower heads. "What are you going to do with these?"

At the gentle question, Blanche's shoulders dropped from her ears. Her face flushed with pleasure and her eyes sparkled. "Oh, I like to make—" and she was off, talking about potpourri, floral beads, and compost.

Sophia smiled with Blanche's enthusiasm. "I love perfume, too," she shared. "I designed my own scents for my hair care back home. I've been thinking of making my own line of products someday."

Blanche's eyes widened, then her face brightened with a lovely smile. She clutched the basket to her chest. "It is fate. I just picked up a perfume still I bought second hand, and I can't wait to try it out. Come over tomorrow after four o'clock and we will use it together." Blanche hesitated, her shyness peeking back through. "If you want to, that is."

"Yes, please. I would love that. Where do you live?"

"Wonderful." Blanche shared the address.

Sophia tapped it into her phone. She had no idea where the location was, but she was sure she could find it. After Blanche got into her rusty car, Sophia stood in the middle of the rose garden, her mouth curving.

This was Fortuna, the goddess of luck. It could be nothing else. The book was right. Her destiny truly was closer than she had thought.

She heard Emelio's voice sneering in her head. "*You want to do too many things, Sophia. You are better off only doing hair instead of all this nonsense with skin and fashion. Let the people who are actually good at it do that.*" He had told her that when she told him of her ideas for adding to her services at the salon. His attitude had crushed her spirit.

Oh, who cared what he thought. He didn't get to have a say in what she did anymore.

Yet, somehow, he still did.

Chapter Four

Learning how to do the things you want counts as progress to making your dreams come true.

How to Take Over the World: Affirmations for Glorious Femmes

Cassie Marks was elbow deep in rolling out pie crust when her brother, Kurt, texted in their family group text: *"HOW DO YOU WASH THE LAUNDRY? HOW DO YOU KNOW WHAT TEMPERATURE OF WATER?"*

Now that she was back in town, her brothers still texted her non-stop, just like they used to do. At least they asked questions instead of demanding that she do their chores for them.

Hands covered in flour, she didn't respond. Within five minutes, the youngest, Lane, texted back: *"Shit, Kurt. Just You-Tube it,"* followed by a string of middle finger emojis.

Grinning, she turned her focus back to making the *Torte della Nonna*—Italian custard tart—for the Café of Hopes and Dreams. Katrina, Edna, and Cassia had agreed to dedicate the next two weeks to Italian food. Tonight, Hiram, Edna's grandson, was upping the stakes by prepping the three and a half pounds *Bistecca alla Fioretina*, a Florentine steak recipe. Since traditional Tuscan beef wasn't available in southern Illinois, he and the butcher in the next town over had gone with the best they could find. Hiram seasoned the meat simply with salt and pepper. He'd told Cassie that he would be basting it with olive-oil-covered rosemary springs and at the end, he'd finish it with a drizzle of balsamic vinegar.

During the afternoon, nearly the whole town had walked by the diner and the bakery, inhaling the aromas of beef, rosemary, and pastries. As a result of Hiram's ambition, Cassie elevated her game, too. Keeping the system she and her lover Nico had developed in Rome, she made two versions of the same dish—a traditional version and one with a modern twist—and made the customers vote between the two. As a result, every student in town staggered about, completely hopped up on sugar.

Sophia clattered down from the apartment above. She peeked into the kitchen and waved at Cassie. "Buongiorno, my darling Cassia." As usual, Sophia looked amazing, even wearing simple blue jeans and a celery-green button-up blouse. Something about the slim gold chain belt and the chain earrings turned her into a goddess. Cassie had learned some Italian style during her stay in Rome, but she still had so much to learn.

Hands in the air to avoid getting flour on her friend's clothes, Cassia leaned toward Sophia for their usual air kisses. "Hello, Sophia." A delicate waft of her perfume teased Cassie's senses. It reminded her of watching the sunsets from her little aerie on the roof of the de Luca's bakery, full of warmth and flowers and cool water. "How are you doing?"

"Confused and fascinated. This whole being alone is very new to me," Sophia answered. "It is so quiet and strange, but beautiful too."

"It will teach you a lot about who you want to be," Cassie laughed. "What are your plans?"

"Today, I start experimenting with products. I want to make my own scents for the hair, but first, I must learn how to make the oils. I want to understand everything about what I am doing." She showed Cassie an empty market basket. "Blanche and I will be playing with a still today. It will be fun."

Cassie blinked. "I thought stills were illegal."

It was Sophia's turn to blink. "They are? But it's only for the oils. How can that be illegal?"

Cassie laughed. "Oh, people make booze with stills, which is regulated by the government. I thought maybe someone was trying to rope you into making illegal moonshine."

Sophia giggled. "Most definitely not. I will leave the moonshine to someone else. Blanche and I are making essential oils. So exciting! I can't wait to observe the process. Can I still borrow your car?"

"Of course. Get some of her raspberries for me. Hiram and I want to make a trifle together."

"I do not believe this Hiram exists," Sophia teased. "I still have not met him."

Cassie wrinkled her nose as she turned her attention back to the pastry. "Now that you aren't sleeping the whole day away, you will see him in the mornings over at Edna's."

"*Meravigliosa.*" Sophia exited the bakery. "See you later, my darling."

Meravigliosa. What did that mean again? She searched her memory for her Italian phrases. Ah, yes. Wonderful. Marvelous. It sounded great in English, but even better in Italian.

Cassie watched Sophia drive away in Eli's old truck. Beau, the mechanic at the gas station, had tuned it until it purred like a happy kitty. Her middle brother, Kevin, had detailed it so it no longer smelled like old fast food and manure. The other day, Cassie visited her family's home for the first time since she'd returned from Rome. With Eli, her father, now in jail, the Mark house had greatly improved. Her mom really spruced up the place. The broken and rusted equipment had either been fixed or towed away. Cassie smiled at the memory of how a giant pile of honey locust brambles had finally been cut away to reveal a not-too-decayed shed.

"It has potential," her mother had said. *"Maybe a tiny house that we could rent out?"*

"That's a great idea," Cassie had told her mother. *"There are lots of people who like to stay in the country when they're on vacation. This would be a nice spot."*

Joan had put her hands on her hips and studied the big house. *"The old place just needs some mending. It would be a very nice bed and breakfast, don't you think? We could use your recipes."*

"Absolutely. We can make a signature scone to serve your guests!"

The Marks were coming out from under their cloud and were ready for their rainbow. And Cassie couldn't wait to see what happened next.

Keys in hand, Sophia strode toward Cassia's truck. She liked how there was lots of parking on Main Street. Parking in Rome was next to impossible. However, all these spaces also meant a lack of business. If there was even more joy, there would be even more people coming to town. Alice, Henry, and Katrina had brought color and vibrancy to the block with their costumes, hats, and food. What could she do to entice more of the public to Gold Coast?

The red, white, and blue barber pole ahead of her sparked an idea. Why not start with joy for the locals? Bring them down here for more of their everyday experiences? From what she saw at the fashion show, very few of them took advantage of the skilled hair dresser they already had. She had seen him handle hair with panache that night.

She stopped to peek in Raymond's door. "Buongiorno, Raimondo," she called. "How are you today?"

The barber looked up from cleaning his shampoo bowls. "Hello, Sophia." His smile barely touched his lips, but it did. "Coming in to see how the working folk are doing?"

She ignored his grim attempt at humor, knowing that if she engaged, he'd derail her thoughts. "What beautiful flowers you have brought in today," she said, referring to the bouquet of purple roses on the counter. "Did you get them from the memorial garden?"

His gaze moved to the large vase and his face softened a little. "No. I, uh, grew them myself."

"No!" She couldn't resist. Entering the shop, she buried her nose in the abundant blooms. "These are so aromatic." Privately, she thought they would make the base of a brilliant and unusual perfume.

He turned back to the sink, scrubbing the already gleaming porcelain. "I call them, *The Betsy*." His back bowed a little, as if he expected her to make fun or dismiss his flowers.

She pursed her lips. They must have been named after Betsy Whittaker, her Nonna's friend who had made such amazing clothes. Oh, there was some heartbreak there, hidden amongst those petals. Fresh on the heels of her own pain, she understood. Her heart hurt for him.

She studied his face in the mirror. The breeze wafted even more of the rich scent of the unusual roses her way. Betsy Whitaker had loved this dour man, had often spoken of him in warm tones. What had a vibrant, worldly woman seen in a small-town barber? Sophia had to do something to help him. Now was the time to bring up her idea.

She paused before speaking again, though. Was she giving away her good ideas again? Would Raymond take the idea and the money and not give her credit? Did she dare bring it up to him?

A little voice in heart asked, *Would Betsy have loved a man who would take advantage of women?*

A little tingle ran down her spine. Neither Nonna nor her best friend Betsy had steered Sophia wrong when she was younger.

"I had a little idea, Raimondo. I think it is rather wonderful. Perhaps we could work together? Could you imagine how we would transform everyone's hair here? They would look so good. Feel so good!"

He glanced back at her, his eyes narrowing as though he thought she pitied him.

"What exactly do you mean?"

"Perhaps, while I am here, we could find a way to let people know that we can help with their grooming and skin care."

He squinted at her. Seeing her open face, he rinsed the sink. "It's hard to get most people to care for themselves here. That could work. I guess."

"It would! I swear, we would do magical things together."

His lip twitched, almost as if he were repressing a smile. "I'll let you use that station over there, if you want." He nodded at the chair she had used for the fashion show. Its leather was a bit cracked, but it still gleamed. The station in front of it was bare as if it sat waiting for the right person to come and use it.

"Oh, thank you." She grinned. "We will have so much fun."

"Fun. Yeah. Huh."

She kept going. "And those flowers you raise are so beautiful. We simply must make a one-of-a-kind perfume out of them, or even a face toner. Men smell amazing in rose cologne. It could be a signature scent for you."

His eyebrows lifted and his mouth dropped. "What?"

Warming to his surprise at how wonderful his flowers were, she continued. "I can see it already. The beard balm could be named, 'Whitaker Wax'. And we would name the cologne after you."

"What, 'The Grumpy Man'?" he scoffed.

"No. It would be, 'The Passionate Man.' That was what Betsy always called you when she visited." She had been very young, but she still remembered Zia Betsy telling Nonna about the man she loved. One day Sophia had asked Zia Betsy what "passionate" meant. Zia had laughed and said, "One day I hope you will learn for yourself."

A splotchy red blush crept over Raymonds's sun-tanned face. "Oh, go on with you." He scrubbed his hands over his eyes, but she saw the glint of a tear between his fingers.

"I will see you later, then." She bit back any further comments so she would not embarrass him.

When she opened the truck door, she glanced back. Raymond had his nose buried in the big bouquet of roses on his counter. She was sorry she had made him cry, but she was not sorry to see him remember his favorite lady.

What would it be like, she thought, to have a love that inspired the slow and tender breeding of a rose variety, rather than to have a love that inspired anxiety?

Chapter Five

Scent is a magic potion that immediately grants confidence.
How to Take Over the World: Affirmations for Glorious
Femmes

The first thing Blanche Sandersen did when she arrived home and the screen door banged shut behind her was kick off her outdoor shoes and line them up neatly next to the back door. She never entered through the front door. Not even once in over twenty years. Ezra had firmly believed the front door was for visitors only.

"That's not for us, Missus," he'd firmly told her the day she moved in with her new husband. She'd started toward the front porch, but he'd steered her down the side of the house

to the back. *"Best to keep our dirt to the back. Don't go planting your herbs out there either. We don't want the neighbors seeing our mess."*

The front porch was one of the best places to plant herbs because it got great sunlight, and honestly, she found them soothing. But she'd done as he said. For twenty years. She'd always done what he said. In fact, it had taken her two years after his death before she managed to put her pots of herbs on the front porch as she'd always wanted. It had been months afterward before she finally realized he wasn't going to pop up and chastise her for mucking up the porch.

But she still came in the back way. Every time.

The second thing she did was slide on her house slippers. She did love those. They were nice and soft as she padded through the kitchen to set her basket of rose dead heads on the counter next to the sink. Ezra had been set against wearing outdoor shoes in the house, although she found that was one thing on which she did agree with him. It cut down on floor cleaning more than you might think.

The final thing she did, before getting to work, was remove the scarf she'd wrapped around her head. She let out a sigh of relief as the cool air teased its way through her tangled hair.

It was so hot out. She'd give almost anything not to wear her scarf, but she never let anyone see her hair. Ever. Not now.

She filled the sink with cool water and dumped in the roses, swishing them around a bit to remove cobwebs, insects, or any other nasties she didn't want. Once they were clean, she gently scooped them out with a strainer and left them on cooling racks. The racks were actually meant to cool cookies, but they worked perfectly to dry out herbs and flowers for her little experiments. And Ezra wasn't here to give her the side-eye and tell her she had no business wasting time with such things.

"We are simple people, Missus. We've no need for fancy pot-poories and fripperies." He never pronounced potpourri right. It drove her crazy, but she was sure he did it on purpose. He might have been a farmer and some people may have looked down their noses at his profession, but he was well read and highly intelligent. But for some reason, he liked to cultivate the "hick farmer" stereotype. Maybe because it made people underestimate him. *"Never let 'em see the real you, Missus. Safer that way."*

Well, she needn't worry about that. She'd ceased to be Blanche the day she'd married Ezra Sandersen. He'd started calling her "Missus" and from then on, so did everyone else in town. In fact, she was pretty sure the entire town had forgotten her real name, despite having known her since birth. Sometimes she felt like she nearly had.

That was the thing about being married to Ezra. She'd loved him, she had. And he'd been a good-hearted man. But he'd had his ways, and one of those ways was *consuming*. That was the best way to describe it. He had such a big personality, he *consumed* everyone's around him. Even hers.

Especially hers.

Her entire identity had become about being someone's wife. Ezra's wife. But he was gone now, taking that identity with him, and now she had no idea what or who she was anymore. In fact, for the most part, she was still just "Missus." Going about life just as she had when Ezra was alive. Doing things his way because that's how he liked it, even though he wasn't here to care one way or the other.

She scooped out another bunch of roses, let the water drain, and spread them gently on the next rack. This was her one rebellion. This and the pots of herbs out front. So, two rebellions, she supposed.

Although was it rebellion if there was no one left to rebel against?

The crunch of gravel and the rumble of a motor shocked her out of her reverie. Sophia was here!

She laid the strainer in the sink and started for the front door. She'd nearly reached it when suddenly she remembered. Her scarf!

Feeling a little faint, she rushed back down the hall to the kitchen and grabbed the cloth, wrapping it almost too tightly around her hair. She quickly checked in the mirror on the back of the kitchen door to make sure her hair was properly covered and let out a sigh of relief. She'd almost revealed her secret shame.

She could almost hear Ezra now, for all that he had been gone for two years now. *"Good lord, Missus. What would you do without me here to make sure you got out of the house looking decent?"*

Clearly, she did not do well. Maybe it was best she was just "Missus," after all.

Sophia climbed the three steps in front of Blanche Andersen's white farmhouse and knocked on the screen door. The aluminum siding left chalky residue on her knuckles. Discreetly, she wiped her hand on her slacks. How strange.

She glanced around the narrow front porch which stretched the entire length of the house. There was no railing, but several galvanized troughs lined the edge, forming a low barrier. The troughs held a riot of fresh growing herbs which perfumed the air: mint, rosemary, sage, thyme, chamomile, and more. Nearly every herb you could imagine grew on Blanche's porch.

Blanche opened the door, her hair up in a light blue scarf. "Please, come in." She smiled, as she held open the screen door, the metal hinges squeaking in protest as if rarely used and annoyed at being woken from their nap.

"Thank you," Sophia murmured, instinctually going for the air kiss. Blanche bumped heads with her but recovered fast enough to for the kiss on the other cheek.

Blanche gave a warm chuckle. "I don't know if I'll ever get used to that, but I like it. Welcome to my home. Follow me." She led Sophia through the small entryway and down the hall. "This is my kitchen."

"What a lovely space," Sophia exclaimed, setting down her basket on the counter, gazing around her in wonder. It was so much bigger than her family's tiny kitchen in Rome.

Blanche's kitchen was an homage to the importance of cooking. A bone saw hung from a rafter, along with a host of other knives and cleavers. Long butcher block counters held boxes of canning jars, cutting boards, and an unfortunately dusty collection of cocktail glassware. She'd placed giant bowls of roses, mint, and freshly cut rosemary on the large oval table.

"Grab the rosemary," Blanche said, "and follow me."

Sophia snagged the bowl of rosemary and followed Blanche out the back door into a magnificent view of abundant plants. An apple tree, a peach tree, and a fig tree spread branches over various vegetables in long, raised beds. More raised beds against the fences kept berry brambles from taking over the yard, although Sophia had no doubt Blanche made use of the brambles, as well. The berries they produced would be delicious.

The ancient Persians had created the word "paradise" to mean a walled area, a pleasure-ground. Blanche Sandersen's garden was the most elevated of places, complete with a seating area of chairs around a cute wrought iron bistro table, and even a hammock strung between two gnarly old pear trees.

"This is a work of art," Sophia breathed. Even the ancients, devotees as they were of parks and *latifundia,* would appreciate this space.

"Thank you." Blanche smiled, clearly proud of the space she'd created. "Over here."

Around the corner, a rustic outdoor kitchen, complete with a gas grill with burners, sat on a concrete pad. A setup worthy of a laboratory sat on the large table. A large glass vessel, about three liters, rested on top of a burner. A round bulb sat on top of the vessel, and a series of tubes led to a beaker resting on the apparatus holding the whole thing upright.

"I've already cleaned the equipment by making distilled water, so we're ready to distill some essential oils. Let's start with that rosemary." Blanche held her hand out for the bowl.

Together, they stood at the sink, swishing the cut rosemary branches through cool water to remove all the dirt.

"I did my research," Sophia commented as they packed the vessel with the cleaned branches. "Rosemary means 'dew of the sea' and symbolizes remembrance."

"I believe it." Blanche bent over the bowl and inhaled deeply. "I used to make these flower waters with a pan with an inverted lid and ice, but I really wanted to see what I could do with a larger arrangement."

They connected the containers together with silicon tubes. Sophia lit the fire on the gas burner, adjusted the flame, and they sat down to watch the process. A short while later, the garden filled with the evergreen aromatic scent, fresh and pungent. Drip by drip, the distillate filled the final receptacle. After an hour, they admired the large clean jar of the fresh hydrosol, a thin layer of the essential oil floating on top.

"It smells amazing out here," Blanche said. "I feel so invigorated." She adjusted the knot on her head scarf, the hair under the scarf moving oddly. Instead of a smooth glide, it shifted like she hid a big ball.

Sophia's gaze stayed on Blanche's head. "Me too. While the mixture is settling, let's use this time to 'play goddess' as my mother puts it."

"What is that?"

"It is when we make ourselves feel amazing. Is pampering the right word? Making ourselves beautiful. Radiant."

Blanche shook her head. "No one has time for that."

Sophia tutted. "You must have time for that. Beauty is not just about the external. Beauty can also be rituals that make you feel good."

Blanche picked at her nails, pulling away a long string of dried cuticle. "Uh. I haven't felt good in a long time," She rubbed her hands together.

"Then let me help you." Sophia patted the teak chair. "You deserve it."

Blanche paused for a moment, looking like a pigeon seeking a place to land amongst a line of hungry cats. Whatever she saw on Sophia's face seemed to reassure her.

Sophia raised her hands to remove Blanche's scarf, and then paused. "May I see your hair?"

Blanche bit her lip. "I bet none of those pretty Italian ladies have hair problems." A tear leaked out of each eye.

"I promise that no matter what you have under there, I will not judge," Sophia soothed. "And even in Rome, women have difficulties."

"I'm ashamed," Blanche whispered, eyes downcast.

Sophia held Blanche's shoulders. "Shame is a weapon meant to keep women from growing."

Chapter Six

Your body is a temple, and you are the goddess within.

How to Take Over the World: Affirmations for Glorious

Femmes

A little color came back to Blanche's face. "Okay." She pulled out the hair pins and unwound the scarf from her head. Her gray-streaked brown hair looked smooth and brushed at the front, some of it falling to her hips. At the nape of her neck, though, the hair tangled into a matted ball the size of both Sophia's fists.

Blanche lifted her chin. "Have at it."

Sophia paused. This was going to take some magic, and she had no doubt her new friend needed that magic. Her fingers tingled as excitement coursed through her at the challenge. "Will you do me the honor of allowing me to care for you?"

Tears pooled in the corners of Blanche's eyes again but she swallowed them down. "I don't know. It's just easier to hide it."

Oh, this woman had been holding herself together with nerves of steel, Sophia thought. She needed to let herself be soft for a little while.

She tangled her fingers in the wad of hair. "Please let me," she murmured. Blanche Sandersen's heartbreak, whatever it was, was hiding here in this angry knot.

"I don't have the money," she protested.

"I can't charge anyway. I'm not licensed in the United States." Sophia laughed. "This is just one friend pampering another. Do say yes. We will make it joyful."

"How could this possibly be joyful?" Blanche sounded doubtful.

"Because learning to feel good is fun. Because finding your inner goddess reminds you of your true self."

Blanche hesitated, her breath catching in her throat on a sob that she didn't quite release. "Alice said that I was Ceres, Goddess of Agriculture."

Sophia smiled, framing Blanche's face with her palms. "Then let us honor her." Combs and scissors weren't magic wands, but she had seen the transformations they could evoke. She moved to stand behind Blanche, studying the hard ball of matted hair. "Now, we could pick this apart. It would take at least several hours, perhaps a day or two. Otherwise, we could cut it out. Either way, I recommend we use the barber shop for some proper scissors and shampooing. If you want to keep it long, I could cut away the split ends and give you some deep conditioning." She lifted the heavy mass, letting air reach Blanche's neck. "And I'd give you lovely face masque, too. That will make for a happy goddess."

Blanche rounded her shoulders. Sophia heard her breathing deeply, her back shaking a little as she repressed more sobs. Gently, she petted Blanche's head, detangling small snarls with her fingers, stroking the long strands. "Let it go," she whispered. "You are safe here."

Sophia didn't know what Blanche had experienced. Had no idea what wounds she carried. She did know, though, from her years of experience in the salon, that many, many women carried the energy of their pain in their hair and scalps. They denied themselves any amount of self-care, even the most basic, as if they had no right to it. As if the care of others were of far more importance than their own, working themselves into shadows of themselves. Aesthetic pleasures affirmed life and were doorways to opening the heart and rediscovering one's true self.

Eventually, the deep peace of the backyard seeped into the crying woman. Blanche straightened her shoulders and took a deep breath.

Sophia joined her, the woodsy scent of the rosemary healing and uplifting her soul as much as it no doubt did for Blanche.

"My late husband never let me cut my hair," Blanche explained softly. "He said he wanted it long enough to wrap around his body, never mind that it gave me headaches. And this is what happened." She craned her head to look at Sophia. Her nose was swollen and red, but her eyes were determined. "It's my turn. I get to look any way I want. Cut it out."

Chapter Seven

Beauty is too important to leave to the critics.

How to Take Over the World: Affirmations for Glorious Femmes

While Blanche was inside the house, splashing her eyes with cold water, Sophia called Raymond. "I have a favor to ask."

"What is it?" he grumbled, yet there was a hint of interest in his tone.

"Blanche needs hair and skin care. Is the barber shop busy now?"

"Who?"

"Blanche. You know, Mrs. Sandersen."

"Oh, Missus S? Sure, come on in." He let out a heavy sigh before he hung up.

Sophia wasn't sure what kinds of favors people usually asked of Raymond, but he surely sounded put upon. Also, how did he not know his friend's first name? Did the whole town call her Missus? As if her entire identity was being a wife of someone?

She shook her head and went back to gathering some of the fresh rosemary water in a screw-top jar. Rosemary stimulated hair growth and helped scalp health, both of which would aid Blanche immensely. She would use it as a rinse after cutting out the tangle and shampooing.

Together, they packed up, including Cassia's berries, and drove into town. The women were silent, each lost in her own thoughts. Blanche's words about it being her turn resonated in Sophia's soul. She pondered why they had given her chills. Perhaps because she'd been in a supporting role with Emelio.

She'd happily surrendered her focus on her own business in order to encourage him. She'd put herself and her business second, and both had suffered. And he'd happily taken advantage, dumping her when she had given him what she had to give and leaving her drained. Her soul was exhausted.

At first, being with Emelio had been a dream of excitement. Sophia was an only child, protected, encouraged but also isolated. In her youth, she and her parents had spent most of their time together. She'd not had too many friends in school since she was usually at home. Since her Mama had a little agoraphobia, they even watched the Lazio and Roma football games at home, not at the stadiums. Emelio's sister and friends were young and loud and active. He had pushed her out of her comfort zone, demanding she join him at the latest night clubs, games, and restaurants.

It had been fun, being part of the beautiful people. Her clothing had gone from classic Italian pieces to fashion that couldn't stand to be washed more than five times. She'd been engulfed in his dream of living fast. She'd loved feeling beautiful. Being Emelio's sexy Roman girlfriend gave her such a buzz, even better than the fancy cocktails and liquors they had consumed.

Those nights, Emelio showered her with fervor, kissing her deeply while the party had spilled into the street, fisting his hands in her hair as he had pushed her up against walls to rub against her.

Her heart sped up a little from remembering his ardor. She had loved feeling so desired. Yes, her next love would have to have some real enthusiasm for love-making.

After six months, she began to droop. She hadn't done well staying out so late. She'd grown up in a bakery, where everyone got up early. Those quiet hours in the morning were where she got her best ideas, before the city revved up to full bustle.

They neared the railroad tracks that separated Gold Coast proper from the surrounding area. "I never knew there was such a thing as a jump-rope championship," she mentioned, staring at the welcome sign.

"Yeah, I was part of that team," Blanche commented. "That sure was a long time ago." She rolled her head to Sophia. "It had been a dream come true, to have all that attention. We met the governor, had our picture up at the high school." She laughed. "I'm pretty sure that's where Eara noticed me first. He objected to my pink zebra-striped leg warmers. Said they were too flashy. I think the kids today call that 'negging.'"

Sophia caught her breath. *"You are too conservative,"* Emelio had told her several times before going out. *"You need to look more up-to-the-minute if you are going out with me."*

It startled her to realize that Emelio's dream had left no room for her to be her true self. She had been in a supporting role, giving his influencer friends haircuts for discounted prices, making other people look good. Making *him* look good.

She loved making people look good. If she centered herself, though, what was her dream?

Putting aside the unsettling thoughts, she parked in front of the café. After dropping off Cassia's berries, they crossed the street and entered the barber shop.

"Hey, Missus S." Raymond nodded as he trimmed Merv's hair.

"Hey back at ya."

Merv, the town doctor, gave Blanche a little, two-finger salute and went back to reading his medical journal.

"I hope you are well." Blanche replied. He grinned.

After Blanche's moment of vulnerability, Sophia could see the strain of maintaining the quiet farm wife mask the town expected. It was all a façade to hide her true pain. Once in the chair with a drape on her, Blanche bit her lips, nervously glancing at Merv and Raymond.

Sophia bent over and murmured in her ear, "I'm sending lots of love to you through every hair I touch. And don't worry. I won't let them see."

The tension lines on Blanche's face eased. Sophia hovered her hands over the scarf. Blanche nodded, her lips pressed together in determination.

So it begins, Sophia said to herself. She unwound the scarf. Quickly and smoothly, she cut the big tangle out and swept it into the garbage. Blanche sighed. Her shoulders dropped. Her breathing deepened.

Sophia smiled to herself. This was the magic a stylist could bring.

With the worst over, she gathered the remaining strands and studied them. The shafts were rough and when she gathered them together, a large number broke, the hair weak and damaged. Oh, this poor woman. Every sad thought, every loss had gathered here.

Well, first things first. She had to remove the dirt and residue. Good thing she had strong fingers to make it through the remaining long tresses. She moved them over to the hair washing station.

Once finished with the shampoo, she poured the jar of rosemary water through the clean hair. Merv and Raymond both inhaled loudly.

"Now that smells great," Merv said. "Reminds me of medical school. A bunch of the alternative types would have rosemary going for study sessions to keep themselves alert."

"Did it work?" Raymond asked.

"Well, none of them used speed to get through it, so it must have." He paid for his cut, put his blazer on, then leaned in close. "It's been a while since you've had your physical, Missus. Give me a call soon." Then louder for the rest to hear, "See ya, Raymond. Good day, ladies." He exited the barber shop and strode purposely toward his office up the street.

Sophia slathered Blanche's head with a thick conditioner. The sun-damaged hair soaked up the moisture. She wrapped a towel around the hair and brought Blanche to the cutting station. "I'm going to let this sit in your hair for about ten minutes."

Blanche pulled out her phone, but Raymond dug around in a drawer and pulled out some bowls and a nail kit. "While that's working, I'll take care of your nails."

Blanche's eyes widened. "You do nails?"

Raymond gave his tiny smile. "I'm a full-service barber, even if most of my clients don't use my full services. I can do a mean classic clip, trim, and buff."

He and Sophia nodded at each other, then he placed Blanche's hands in bowls of warm, soapy water. She sighed and closed her eyes.

After Sophia cleaned the sink, she grabbed a wide-toothed comb and smoothed out the wet hair. Every movement was slow and gentle so as not to cause more damage.

Silently, she and Raymond worked in unison. Despite his grumpy exterior, he tenderly washed their client's hands. He stopped to rub at a spot on the webbing between Blanche's thumb and forefinger. She gave a quiet sigh, relaxing even further into the chair.

Once all the small tangles were out, Sophia whispered, "How short would you like your hair?"

"This seems so frivolous," Blanche responded, her eyes still closed. "I have so much to do, I don't really have time for styling. I'm really not worthy of all this attention."

"Beauty rituals are the most magical and efficient way to re-invent yourself." Sophia ran her fingers over Blanche's scalp and forehead. "Feeling good is neither insignificant nor frivolous. It is important."

Raymond cleared his throat. "Missus S has had a hard time. Her husband died about two years ago."

Sophia stroked Blanche's cheeks, imagining her loving parents bereft of each other. "Such a sadness."

Blanche sucked in a deep breath. "Cut it to my shoulders, then do what you want. It's time to start over."

Chapter Eight

"What do you want? Do you believe you deserve it?"
How to Take Over the World: Affirmations for Glorious
Femmes

Raymond took his tools back to his station to clean and sanitize them. In that moment of privacy, Sophia rested her hands on the top of Blanche's head, letting warmth grow on the tense scalp. Slowly, tight muscles twitched and loosened.

"What do you want in life?" she asked. "Where do you want to go from here?"

"I tried for years to be my highest self." Blanche slid her hands from under the styling cape and made air quotes around 'highest'. Her lips twisted a little, creating a bitter smile.

"That's what Ezra always talked about. 'Don't be angry, Missus. Listen to your highest self.'" She sighed as though she tossed a heavy suitcase full of broken glass over her head. "It exhausted me. All I did was give. I gave away my best crops because that is what a good person is supposed to do. I did all the housework because that's what a good wife did." She lifted her chin and looked at Sophia in the mirror. "I want to be happy with myself. I want to be playful and silly and have fun and adorn myself and...." She took a deep breath and straightened her spine. "I want to make money off my labor."

"Yes." Sophia cheered. "Those are good wants. You deserve them all." In fact, Blanche's dream looked really good to Sophia herself.

"I believe that I do," Blanche stated, lifting her chin a little. "I believe it and I want it and I deserve it."

"You are not alone. Together, we can make it happen." With that, Sophia picked up the scissors and the comb. "Let us see who you really are."

She started with cutting the perimeter of Blanche's hair, gradually working shorter and shorter until it was shoulder length. With each snip, a light curl began to reveal itself. The weight of the length had pulled that nice bounce flat. Once the length was right, she opened the straight razor.

Blanche's eyes widened at the blade.

"Your hair will love this," Sophia assured her. "I will slice away all of these dead ends, lightening up the main mass. It will also cut away all the sadness in your locks, leaving you full of joy."

"If you say so," Blanche murmured, but there was a slight twist to her lips, the beginnings of a smile. It was clear she was already feeling lighter and brighter.

With each pass of the razor, Sophia could almost see the sorrow and stuck grief leave Blanche's body. Her spine straightened in a relaxed, easy manner instead of forcing herself upright against the pressure pushing her down. The skin at the corners of her eyes smoothed out. The wrinkles around her mouth softened, leaving her with a tiny smile.

"Oh, I'm liking it so far."

"Good."

Sophia saw Raymond in the mirror. His head was tipped to one side. His eyes narrowed at how she used the razor, and his hands traced the same movements she made. Her heart melted. How kind of him to learn from her. So many older men refused to be open to new ideas, especially from women.

Emelio was open to her ideas, but he had not acknowledged her knowledge. Instead he'd stolen them and taken the glory and success for himself.

She shoved the thought away. It would not do to lose concentration when using a straight razor.

Blanche's curls revealed themselves, framing her face with vitality. The gray blended in with the once-faded brown to give her sparkle. Sophia took some of Raymond's gel, worked it through, then dried and styled the hair with a diffuser. Using small shears, she nipped away the wiry stray hairs on Blanche's eyebrows, revealing a strong, dark brow with an excellent natural shape.

"Can I see?" Blanche asked eagerly.

Sophia narrowed her eyes a little, studying her friend's face and hair. "For a proper goddess day, I would like to give you a facial cleansing massage. That will really give you a glow-up."

"I've never had one."

"That is a crime against womanhood," she teased.

While the women bantered, Raymond laid out cleanser, a scrub, and hot towels in a blue ceramic bowl. "There you go," he murmured.

"Thank you." Sophia smiled at him. "You are a very generous man and I appreciate your help."

Raymond's jaw dropped, then another bright red blush traveled up his neck and cheeks. "Uh, it's nothing." He grabbed his phone and slunk away to sit in the other chair.

Shrugging, she turned back to Blanche. "Shall we?"

"Let me see," Blanche whispered after the last hot towel had been lifted away.

"Wait a second." Reaching for her purse, Sophia pulled out a gold filigree compact. With her fingers, she patted some of the soft gold-pink powder on Blanche's cheeks. Her newly cleansed and exfoliated skin looked fresh and bright. One last fluff of the bangs and... perfect. "Close your eyes."

Blanche obeyed. Sophia spun Blanche around. "Take a look."

Blanche's eyelids flew open. A second passed before she gasped. "Oh. My. God. Is that *me*?" She stood out of the chair and leaned into the mirror. "I can't believe it."

Instead of a long, matted, broken mess, shiny brown and silver curls draped down her shoulders. When she shook her head, it bounced and moved around her. Her skin, once dull from sun and dry skin, shone with a healthy glow.

"I look like...."

Raymond's and Sophia's gazes met, and they smiled. They both understood the power of care rituals.

"A goddess, yes. Behold, your favorite self." Sophia removed the cape and shook the trimmings out. "Your hair is like a Louis Vuitton bag. Care for it and it will be the best accessory you have."

Blanche touched her face, her expression one of wonder. "I feel reborn."

Chapter Nine

A dream dies to make room for another, brighter one.

***How to Take Over the World: Affirmations for Glorious
Femmes***

"**M**issus," Katrina Kennedy-Pentecost cried out from behind the counter of The Café of Hopes and Dreams. "You look amazing!"

Cassie looked up from her laptop and hollered, "Woohoo! Girl!"

"Holy shit, darling." Edna's mocha cup clattered in the saucer as she nearly dropped it.

Alice Kennedy, the owner of The Dream Factory, looked away from her hand-sewing, and gave out a wolf-whistle.

Even the three high school boys picking up bear claws gave her a thumbs up.

Not since she had gotten married had Blanche had so much positive attention. It felt good. Really good, like the appreciation soothed a wound so old, she had forgotten about it.

Standing in the door, Blanche tossed her new hair from side to side. "Sophia did it."

"She is a genius, isn't she?" Cassie said. "It's amazing what she can do." She fluffed her own hair. "She saw the real me and brought her forth."

"Nice line, Cassie," Katrina observed.

Cassie made a little, 'it was nothing' gesture and went back to her writing. Blanche hoped it was a new entry for her food blog. She'd thoroughly enjoyed those posts even before she knew it was Cassie who wrote them. She'd even tried some of the recipes.

"What will you have, Missus?" Katrina asked from her position behind the counter. She glowed with health and vitality and the happiness and joy of love.

"I'll have a Viennese cinnamon coffee. With whipped cream. I always wanted to try one of those." She approached the counter. "And please, call me Blanche, instead. Ezra is gone." She wasn't sure why she added that last part. Katrina hadn't known Ezra. She'd have no way of knowing he was the one who'd started calling her Missus.

Katrina smiled. "You got it, Blanche." She filled a pretty mug at the Air-Pot that was marked with today's special coffee. "Here."

"Hey, good job, Sophia," Edna called.

"Thank you," Sophia answered from the door.

Blanche could see Sophia's reflection in the polished glass of the display case. She grinned at the sight of fashionable Sophia in the wavy, old glass. Like a funhouse mirror, it elongated the girl's forehead to outrageous heights, then squished her down to look like a cartoon character. In the glass, she saw Sophia frown down at her phone.

Despite the distortion, Blanche could see the slight droop in Sophia's shoulders, a hesitation in the way she stood in the doorway. She turned around. "Come on in, my dear. You deserve a treat, too. You did all the work."

With that, Sophia entered the café with confidence and snap, but there were faint fatigue lines at the corners of her eyes and a stiffness to her stride that hadn't been there earlier. Blanche recognized the signs of hidden stress from what she had seen in her own mirror the last two years. The Roman beauty looked like she had the world on a string, but she was hurting inside. After the hard work she had just done showing Blanche her inner radiance, there was nothing she wouldn't do for the young woman. She wasn't yet sure what Sophia needed, but she was going to figure it out and help her new friend the way Sophia had just helped her.

"I'll have a *caffé*," Sophia said. At Katrina's confused look, she added, "Just a shot of espresso."

Katrina started working with the sleek black machine with its mysterious handles and spouts. "Anything else?"

Cassie said, "Try the Torta Antiqua, Sophia. I just made it."

"An excellent suggestion." Sophia gathered her food and smiled at Blanche. "Shall we sit?"

"Come here," Cassie suggested. "You two look like you have something on your minds."

The teenaged boys exited, sitting on the café chairs on the sidewalk. Once they were gone, the women in the town clustered around Cassie's table. Katrina circled the counter with ordered cups of hot coffee in her hand.

Blanche looked around the table. Every woman here owned their own business. Not only that, they were happy *and* making money. *I could ask for some ideas,* Blanche thought. If her dream was to be rewarded for her labor, these other entrepreneurs could be her allies.

Instead of waiting for Sophia to speak, Blanche piped up. "I was telling Sophia that I want to play more. Have fun. And..." She flattened her palms on the table, gathering her courage. Putting herself out there was hard, but she was going to do it anyway. "I want to start selling my harvests." Nervous, she sipped her Viennese coffee. The combination of milk, coffee, and cinnamon cut through her nerves. What if she was asking too much from the people who had benefited from her freebies?

Katrina's gaze fuzzed out, as if she were looking at something only she could see. "I know what you need. And it will help the whole town. What about a farmer's market in the empty shop next door?"

Blanche's eyes widened. She had not expected such an enthusiastic response so quickly.

Edna nodded. "That is a great idea."

"You could sell whatever you did that made you both smell so good," Cassie added.

"We made hydrosols and some oils today," Sophia responded.

"Oh, yeah," Katrina added enthusiastically. "I can see it. Scented soaps and lotions, some perfume, even skin toner."

Cassie tipped her head to Sophia. "This would be the perfect place sell hair care."

Edna licked a drop of mocha off the back of her hand. "You know who would be a great help? Kailani Jones."

Alice raised her eyebrows, asking silently who Kailani was.

Edna sighed. "The girl who runs the dairy farm just outside of town. She was just telling me how much she'd love to have a place to sell all her products. She raises chickens, too, so she'd have eggs." A grin crossed Edna's face. "I'd love to have her stuff nearby and not have to go to the farm to get ingredients."

Excitement sizzled around the table. It had been a long time since there'd been a grocery store in town. The only one had closed down almost two decades ago, driven out of business by the big box stores in the nearby towns.

"It would make a wonderful addition," Blanche blurted. "Instead of having to go away for groceries, we could do quick shopping right here on Main Street. Especially fruits and vegetables. Books and Bait sells some small stuff, but this would carry more."

Sophia tossed back her espresso shot. "The women here are unstoppable," she laughed. "Let's go look at the place."

Blanche raised her eyebrows at the potential store. Surprisingly, it was clean, with big sparkling windows, and a stark white interior. Knotted wood shelves lined the walls. "Wasn't this the old video shop?"

Enda nodded. "Remember, Owen ran it until he changed businesses over to Books and Bait? He told me the market dropped out of VHS rentals a while ago and he wanted a more recession-proof establishment."

Alice nodded. "People always need books."

"And bait," Katrina snorted. The sisters cracked up.

Blanche remembered. The last time she'd been here had been almost a decade ago when Owen had his going out of business sale. Although he'd called it a "diversification sale." She'd almost bought the video of one of her favorite films with Colin Firth, *Pride and Prejudice.* But at the last minute, she'd decided it was too frivolous and had left without it. She'd always regretted that.

Maybe she'd check and see if she could get the movie on one of the streaming channels. She could make some popcorn and watch it tonight. The thought was so decadent, she almost felt guilty.

But why should she feel guilty over a movie night? What was so wrong about that?

Treat yourself, Blanche. You deserve it.

"What do you think of the place?" Edna asked Blanche, startling her out of her thoughts.

"I think it might work. Sophia?" She glanced over her shoulder at Sophia for her opinion, but the girl still stood outside, frowning again at her phone. What did such a young, accomplished, smart woman have to be so sad about?

Sophia wiped her eyes. Her shoulders hunched in as if she were rolling in on herself like a pillbug.

Oh. Blanche recognized that look. That was the look of a woman trying not to cry over a man. The last two years, she did it so much herself, trying not to cry over Ezra. She spun her head back around, returning her attention to her other friends who were already labeling where things would go in the new store.

Look at the lines outside the restaurant! Emelio had texted her a picture of the front of Greco's. It was long, but not as long as it was before he'd dumped her. *Send more ideas immediately.*

Rage swamped her, filled her eyes with frustrated tears.

Who the hell did he think he was? That she would just blithely give over more of her time and energy to someone who didn't respect her? To someone who broke his promises? To someone who had dumped her?

She wiped at her eyes.

When her vision cleared, she saw that the words on her phone had changed. Instead of his demanding message, she read, *"A lawyer's time and advice are his stock in trade,"* Abraham Lincoln.

The words struck her like a splash of cold water. What in heaven's name? Where did that come from? Her phone read, Unknown Number at the top of the text, so there was no way her ex had sent that. How did she get a comment out of nowhere, from no one, that was able to give her the exact help she needed in the moment?

She sent a text back: *WHO IS THIS?*

Her phone pinged again. This time the text was a single angle emoji.

For a moment, she could swear she smelled her Nonna's Officina di Santa Maria Novella Patchouli Eau de Cologne amongst the scents of chocolate and cinnamon. Sophia's longing for her grandmother's hugs wiped away her shock and pain of Emelio's demand.

She shook her head, but the text stayed. Her brain offered something that Cassia had said late one night while they were talking.

"I can't live in Gold Coast, but it is weird and special. Like we have a guardian angel."

At the time, Sophia had nodded, understanding about kind messengers. A person didn't live near Vatican City without believing in things unseen. Still, it was quite surprising when it happened to her. She had her own guardian angel looking after her, perhaps her Nonna or Aunt Betsy.

The message made her stop and think about Emelio's message. Her Nonna used to snap, "Samples are for people who buy the cookbook," when people asked her for free pastries.

It had always amused Sophia, but Nonna was right. Why would she give advice to someone who wouldn't pay her? Who wouldn't even acknowledge her contribution?

She shoved her phone into her pocket, determined to ignore any and all texts from Emelio, and strode into the empty storefront. "My dears," she asked the women gathered in the center of the room. "What is the word for someone who gives business recommendations?"

"A consultant," Katrina answered.

Consultant. The word tasted like sweet whipped cream on her tongue. Sophia felt a satisfied smile curl her lips. Yes. No more would she give away her stock in trade. Starting today, she would form another empire of love. Of course, right now, it was an empire of one, but like the story of Horatius at the bridge, one person could make a giant difference.

Chapter Ten

Sunscreen, fresh foods, a signature scent, and a gorgeous shade of lipstick are the basic necessities of beauty for a femme.
How to Take Over the World: Affirmations for Glorious Femmes

S ophia and Cassia draped themselves over the sofa in the apartment above the bakery. The warm fall day was slowly cooling off to night. They clinked their second glasses of chilled amaretto and sipped. The view out of the front window showed them the lights coming up on Main Street.

"This street used to be so sad," Cassia murmured. "Most of the buildings shuttered and empty. Half the streetlights burned out. Not a spot of color anywhere. Now look at it."

Loops of white lights draped from lamppost to lamppost, giving the street a magical glow and reflected off freshly washed windows. Long oval metal tubs, filled with hot pink and purple fuchsias, miniature sunflowers, and creeping thyme, provided color and scented the night air.

"It is pretty," Sophia agreed. Yes, there were still a few boarded-up buildings with faded For Rent signs, but she had a feeling those spaces wouldn't be empty for long.

Earlier in the evening, Sophia had made dinner: a light repast of grilled eggplant topped with tomatoes and cheese. Now, it was time to discuss their day.

"How was the writing?" she asked.

"Good. Today I worked on my novel after baking in the morning. It felt like the words really flowed," Cassia answered. "Hey. Did you see the latest review of Il Dolci di Paradisio?"

"No! What is it?"

"Here. It's from a British ex-pat living in Rome site." Cassia handed over her phone, open to the post.

Il Dolci di Paradisio continues its renaissance. The side-by-side comparisons of different versions of their treats have won over the town. The bakery, famous for its espresso and pastries, is now showcasing 'Pastries of the World' once every two weeks. They have shown off their abilities with a Sacher Torte and a Japanese cheesecake. Both sold out within hours. When asked for a comment, Ivy de Luca, the American-born wife of Leonardo de Luca, said, "We are so happy that the people of Rome love good food."

"How wonderful," Sophia sighed, handing Cassie back her phone. Too bad stupid Emelio and his stupid texts got in the way of her seeing the good news. Speaking of which... "Did I show you this earlier?" She handed over her own phone open to Emelio's texts.

"What a jerk." Cassia snorted. "Wait a minute. Is that why you asked about consultants?"

"Yes." Sophia grinned. "He can have my ideas only if he pays for them."

Cassia rubbed her hands together like an evil cartoon character. "What else have you thought of today?"

Leaning over, Sophia opened a tote bag. "Blanche and I made up some homemade foot lotion today." She opened the little glass jar and held it under Cassie's nose. "Peppermint and some lavender."

"Hand it over," Cassie demanded. "My feet are killing me."

Sophia breathed deeply as Cassia rubbed the lotion into her feet and lower legs. The fresh peppermint aroma filled the room, making the lingering heat of the day feel less oppressive. As the lotion warmed up on the skin, the lavender oils bloomed, adding a clean and relaxing scent to the evening. Combined with the ice-cooled amaretto, the little apartment became a sanctuary against all that worried her.

Anger at Emelio's entitlement? Gone. Concern for her parents? Eased. Fear for her financial future? That could wait until she was more rested.

This was what beauty and luxury truly meant, she mused to herself as Cassia moaned in relief. These things were not about money. They meant pauses in everyday life that made dealing with distress easier.

In fact, she would define luxury as the time to subtract all the things that added up and overwhelmed. It allowed one's brain to slow down and be able to find solutions easier later on.

This was her calling, she knew. To help women find the tools that gave them permission to care for themselves.

Chapter Eleven

If pampering brings peace of mind, then pamper away!
How to Take Over the World: Affirmations for Glorious Femmes

Two days later, Sophia perched on one of the dining chairs, staring at the laptop open on the table. She'd ignored every text Emelio had sent. Not engaging had been such a relief. The kitchen window was open, and the cool, early morning breeze fluttered the sheer curtains, carrying the sweet call of songbirds and yeasty scent of bread warm from the ovens below. Cassia was already hard at work, helping Katrina with the bakery. Sophia would go down in a minute to grab some breakfast before she joined her new friends to plan the farmers market, but she had something important to do first.

She opened her email and clicked the "compose" button. After inserting the correct address, she began writing.

Dear Mr. Greco, she began, a little smile curving her lips at how delightfully formal it sounded.

I understand you are interested in obtaining my services as a consultant for your business. As you know, I have a great deal of experience in this area and have proven my abilities time and again to your benefit.

She almost snickered at that one. To the world around, Emelio loved to pretend he was the smart one, the one with the grand ideas, but not a single successful idea had been his. It was all her. And he knew it. Now she did, too.

I would be happy to work with you again in this capacity. Below is a quote for my services.

Her fingers flew as she listed her hourly rate along with a list of services. Marie had helped her at the library, researching just how much her knowledge was worth. Sophia was not going to fall into the trap of devaluing herself. Her smile broadened as she signed off, including her new consultant title. A shiver of pride went through her as she hit send.

Emelio was going to—what was that quaint American term her mama always used?—blow a basket? No. Gasket. Blow a gasket. She wasn't sure what that was, but she had a pretty good idea what it would look like, and she couldn't help feeling a tiny bit of pleasure at Emelio's anger and discomfort. After all, the man had been using her for his own ends for all the time they'd been together. It was time for him to pay the piper, as Mama would say.

Maybe he would hire her or maybe he wouldn't. Frankly, she was fine either way. But she wasn't giving him her expertise for free anymore.

She rose from the table and carefully closed the laptop. She would celebrate with a delicious pastry for breakfast.

As she made her way down the stairs that led from the apartment to the bakery, the scent of baked goods intensified, and she suddenly felt a pang of homesickness. It reminded her so much of her family's café. Of course, this time of day in Rome, the baking would be done, and business would be winding down post lunch. Soon Mama and Papa would head upstairs for a much-deserved rest while her cousin, Nico, cleaned the kitchen in preparation for tomorrow.

In fact, as she stepped into the kitchen of The Café of Hopes and Dreams, she could almost swear she heard Nico's voice.

She peered over the baking rack partially blocking her view and spotted Cassie kneading some dough while above her perched an iPad, Nico's face front and center on the screen.

"I miss you, *cara mia*," he said.

"I miss you, too," Cassie answered. "I love being home, but baking isn't half as fun without you."

Not wanting to interrupt their private time, Sophia slipped out of the kitchen and into the café. Katrina waved at her from behind the counter. She waved back, eyeing the pastry case.

"Morning, Sophia. How's it going?" Katrina wore a wide smile and a pink and white striped apron over a cute 50s-style fit and flare dress. Sophia was betting it was one of Alice's creations.

"It is going very well, Katrina. Thank you." She beamed. "I'm having a little celebration this morning."

Katrina raised a brow. "Oh, really? That's fantastic. What are you celebrating?"

Sophia didn't want to go through the gory details of her relationship with Emelio so she kept it simple. "I stood up for myself to someone with whom I find it difficult to do so."

"Well, that definitely deserves a celebration," Katrina agreed. "Cassie decided to try her hand at *pasticciotto* this morning. They're ridiculously yummy."

"That sounds perfecto. Thank you, Katrina."

"No problem. I'll bring one right out along with some coffee."

Sophia took a seat at one of the tables in the window overlooking Main Street. She enjoyed people watching, and while Gold Coast was no Rome, there were still things to see even early in the morning.

Across the street, Raymond was sweeping his perfectly clean front stoop. He scanned the street as if on the lookout for criminal activity or juicy gossip. If she craned her neck, she could see a young man cleaning the windows of Edna's Diner. That must be the elusive Hiram. He was certainly handsome and full of energy, she thought. An elderly woman she hadn't seen before strolled by with a little cream-colored dachshund on a pink leash. They'd obviously been to the rose garden because the woman clutched a small bouquet of white and pink roses in her other hand. She had matched her dog. How cute!

"Here you go." Katrina interrupted her thoughts as she placed a plate in front of her, along with a steaming mug of coffee. "Mind if I join you?"

"Of course not. Please." Sophia beamed, waving to the chair across from her. "I would love that."

Katrina grabbed her own food and coffee and sank down into her chair with a sigh. "I could use a break and a bite. I was up far too late last night."

"I hope it was for something good."

Katrina grinned. "Marie and I are adding a bath house to our caboose."

Sophia blinked. "Your what?"

Katrina laughed. "You know, a caboose. From the end of a train? We live in one. Marie converted it into a tiny house. We love it, but we need more room for a proper bathroom. So we decided to add a bath house. I mean, why not?"

"Why not, indeed." Sophia dug into the *pasticciotto.* It was still warm from the oven, just as she liked them, the short crust crumbly and just a little sweet. The egg custard was creamy and rich with the sharp bite of lemon cutting through the sweetness. Honestly, it was one of the best that she'd ever had, and she'd eaten a lot of these tarts. But she shouldn't be surprised. Cassie performed magic in the kitchen.

"I wanted to thank you," Katrina said, taking a sip of coffee.

Sophia's eyes widened in surprise. "Thank me? For what?"

Katrina nodded toward the kitchen. "For what you've done for Cassie."

"But I've done nothing."

"Oh, you've done a great deal," Katrina insisted. "I've never seen Cassie look so confident. So happy and beautiful."

"She has always been beautiful," Sophia said stubbornly. "I may have helped with hair and makeup, but I can't bring out anything that isn't already there."

"Exactly." Katrina grinned. "You showed her just how beautiful she is. Your friendship and support brought out the best in her. She was headed that way, like a rose bud just starting to unfurl. But you helped her blossom. To realize her potential. And we are all so grateful to you for that."

Sophia shrugged. "Cassie is my friend. What else would I do? Besides, this is what I love."

"Helping other women realize their potential?"

"Yes," Sophia agreed. "And their beauty, both inside and out."

Katrina eyed her over the rim of her coffee mug. "I imagine that's a difficult thing."

Sophia thought it over. "Not so difficult. You simply must listen. And then you must give her a safe space to express herself. She does the rest."

Katrina studied Sophia's face, her eyes crinkled as in thought. "Listening takes energy. Making a safe space takes energy," she said slowly. Reaching out to take Sophia's hand, she continued. "What do you do to renew your energy? What do you like to do when you aren't working? What dreams give you the resources it takes to do what you love?"

Sophia started when she realized her jaw was hanging open. "But isn't doing what we love enough to keep us lit up?"

"When I was married to my ex-husband, I thought that I should be this smiling, ever abundant aquifer, you know? That I never needed my pump primed, that I never needed to test the water or make sure no one had tossed garbage in. I was supposed to be...without needs, I guess. Just always able to produce endlessly."

Sophia widened her eyes in astonishment. Had any woman discussed what the world wanted from them so clearly?

"But we all have needs. We got to take care of ourselves. What fills you up, Sophia?"

Sophia clasped her fingers together. "I had a wonderful time when Blanche and I made the scents together."

"Wonderful," Katrina crowed. She snagged a mini-notebook from the counter. "Here. Eat your breakfast and dream up your life."

"Oh, thank you," Sophia breathed.

Katrina nodded and took a bite of her *pasticciotto.* "This is amazing. I'm going to have to get Cassie to teach me how to make these. The minute Raymond gets ahold of one of these, I won't be able to keep them in stock."

Sophia glanced out the window and laughed. "Speaking of. Guess who is coming this way."

"I guess I better tell Cassie to bake some more of these bad boys." She polished off her tart and then hurried toward the kitchen just as Raymond pushed his way inside. "Be right with you, Mayor."

"Ain't the mayor," Raymond muttered, but his shoulders straightened, and his chin lifted with just a hint of pride.

"Good morning, Mayor Raimondo," Sophia said, following Katrina's lead.

"Mornin', Sophia. And it's just Raymond."

"Raimondo is the Italian version. Isn't it delightfully masculine?"

A hint of pink flushed along his cheekbones. "It's alright I guess." He peered at her plate. "What are you eating?"

"*Pasticciotto.*"

He blinked. "What now?"

"It's an Italian pastry. Like a custard tart. We eat them warm for breakfast. This one is lemon."

His eyes lit up. "I do love me some lemon."

She waved to Katrina's vacated seat. "Then why don't you sit with me and enjoy some? Cassia is making one fresh right now."

"Well, alright then." He sat down and shifted a little as if uncomfortable. Then he blurted, "You want to use my extra chair?"

She felt like she'd come into the middle of the conversation. "Your...chair?"

"Yeah. The extra one in the shop. Since you can't officially set up a business here yet or charge, I figured you could make that side of the shop your own for your volunteer work. I've got some shelves I can put up for you so you can display your little potions and whatnot. And you can use the chair for your treatments and such. You can post your hours in the window if you like."

"Well, thank you, Raimondo. That is very kind of you." He said yes! It was the beginning of her new way of doing business.

"I was thinking about Betsy after you left. She told me she'd created a space where she would play and experiment without worrying about what other people thought." He shrugged as if it were nothing. "Your art needs a space, too." Then he reached into his pocket and placed a key on the table. "Just in case I'm not there and you need to use the place. Just keep your side clean, that's all I ask. Deal?"

She stared at the key, then at him. A slow smile spread across her face to match the warmth spreading through her heart. "Deal."

Raymond didn't know it, but he had just given her a safe space for her dreams. She would make the people of Gold Coast wonder why they should stick to plain when they could have fancy.

Chapter Twelve

Boundaries are like pops of color on an outfit. They fit every woman.

How to Take Over the World: Affirmations for Glorious Femmes

After she finished her custard, Sophia went outside to eye the old storefront that would soon house the farmers' market. It looked...empty.

No problem. All the vendors Blanche had found could fix that. In a way, fixing a building wasn't that different from fixing a woman. All it needed was a little freshening up. A spritz of something special to make it come alive again.

White. She wasn't always a fan of it—preferring color and plenty of it—but it was clean and fresh and would stand out among the red brick buildings and faded store fronts. The trim would be black. The stark contrast between the two would make the shop pop. A black and white sign with just a splash of color would catch the eye. Planters out front—something rustic from Blanche's garden, perhaps—would overflow with a riot of colorful flowers and sweet-smelling fresh herbs to draw customers in.

She nodded. Yes, that was perfect. She'd present it to the other women and see if they had other suggestions.

Her phone vibrated in her pocket, indicating a text. She pulled it out and stared at the screen, a lump forming in her throat.

WHAT IS WRONG WITH YOU?

The text was from Emelio, and the capital letters made it feel like he was screaming at her from all the way in Italy. She could feel her shoulders tense and rise toward her shoulders, but then she forced them back down. No, he had no right to speak to her like this.

She quickly tapped out: *What do you mean? Do you have an issue with my business proposal?*

She took a deep breath and pressed send. Part of her was nervous, knowing he'd be angry. Another part of her felt almost giddy. His anger was not her problem. She was a businesswoman and Emelio was no longer anything more than a potential client. If he didn't like that, then too bad.

She didn't have long to wait.

DO YOU THINK THIS IS FUNNY?

She really didn't. She'd given him so much of herself and instead of being thankful, he'd taken advantage and become more and more demanding. He'd even tried to destroy her family's café so that he could get his hands on more that was not his.

After a moment, she responded: *If you don't like my fee structure, then feel free to hire someone else. Please send all further inquiries via email.*

There. That was professional.

Then she did something else she'd never have thought she was capable of doing. With trembling hands, she blocked his calls and texts. If he hired her, she could unblock him, but until then, he wasn't her problem, and she was done making herself available to him. Her time and energy were valuable. That was something Cassie had taught her.

She exhaled, imagining all the frustration and anger blowing out of her and flying away. Oh, that felt good, like she could move her shoulders and neck freely. She breathed deeply a few more times to enjoy the sensation.

"Sophia!" Someone shouted to her from up the street.

She turned and spotted Blanche striding her way. Sophia blinked, almost not recognizing her friend for a moment. Blanche's hair curled around her face in a delightful riot of beachy waves, the early morning sun glinting off strands of silver shot through her hair like glitter. She wore a bohemian-style smock dress in gorgeous turquoise and greens. It fluttered around her calves, showing off skin still tanned from the summer working in her garden. Her shoulders were back, head up, and she walked with purpose and pride.

Raymond poked his head out of the barber shop and his jaw dropped.

"Morning, Raymond," Blanche said cheerfully.

He cleared his throat. "Morning, Miss— uh, Blanche. Looking good."

"Thank you."

His cheeks turned red, and he disappeared back inside.

"He's right," Sophia said as Blanche approached. "You look amazing."

"I feel amazing." Blanche beamed, her eyes bright, her skin glowing with health. She looked ten years younger than she had when Sophia first met her.

"Good." Sophia beamed back. "I'm happy you feel that way. You are a wonderful person, and you deserve to look and feel good."

Blanche's cheeks turned pink, and her smile widened. "I have you to thank for it."

Sophia shook her head. "I was just the facilitator. You were the one who had to open your heart to possibility."

"Well, I'm wide open." Blanche giggled. "Now, speaking of possibility, how are we going to make this place shine?" She turned to face the empty building that would soon house the market.

"Well, here is what I was thinking for the outside." Sophia shared her ideas and Blanche nodded with excitement.

"I love that! I think black and white will look really good, especially once we plant lots of flowers out front. What about galvanized buckets? They're rustic, but also fun and a bit chic right now. It will give the place a farm feel, but fancy with the flowers."

Sophia wasn't entirely sure she knew what a galvanized bucket was, but she nodded. She trusted Blanche. "I am certain that will look amazing."

They chatted for a bit about other ideas, Sophia occasionally jotting notes in her new little notebook. Then they went inside and brainstormed some more. When they were done, they had several "action items" as Blanche called them, starting with giving the space a final cleaning.

"I'll call around and schedule a day," Blanche suggested.

Sophia nodded. "I'll speak to Raymond about the best place to get buckets and price display items. He might also know someone we can bribe to help set up."

Blanche lifted a brow. "Bribe?"

"We're on a tight budget," Sophia pointed out. "Surely bribing a person with baked goods and hair styling is the way to go." In this town, there were plenty who could use a good cut and some styling products. Not to mention, Cassie would be thrilled to do her part by baking something.

"True," Blanche agreed. "I'll ask around as well. I bet we can get some help easily. Now, why don't you come back to my place? I made biscuits fresh this morning and I've got homemade butter and fresh honey from my hives."

"That sounds amazing." Sophia grinned. This was exactly what she needed in her life. Friends, a community, and a way to share her gifts with the world.

The rest of the day passed quickly as she and Blanche made plans and called contacts.

Not once did she think about Emelio.

Chapter Thirteen

"What do I want?" is the most important question to ask your-self.

How to Take Over the World: Affirmations for Glorious Femmes

The next day at dawn, Sophia wandered into the rose garden with a thermos of coffee and the notebook Katrina had given her. She wiped the dew off one of the picnic tables with an extra cloth napkin, and spread a green and white striped tablecloth over the wooden top. Pouring herself a cup, she settled at the table. If she was going to brainstorm, she would do it right.

Today, she wanted to dream about what she needed. She clicked the ballpoint pen a few times and wrote in big letters in the middle of the paper:

WHAT DO I WANT?

Just seeing it there in purple ink made her catch her breath. She imagined her Nonna, her mother, all the generations of women before her, sitting down and asking themselves this question.

A rush of ideas came at her, as if her soul had been waiting for her to ask this. Rather than try to make sense of them all, she just wrote them all down, as fast as she could.

What are my boundaries? Pay me for my knowledge/know how much my expertise is worth.

She looked down at her hands. Her own skin was looking a touch dry and tight. That stimulated a new idea.

Self-care does not equal neglecting others. Neglecting myself does not mean I'm caring for others.

I want to lift and nurture my soul.

She looked over the colors and the glossy green leaves of the rose garden. The spicy scent of late-blooming roses teased her nose, spinning their magic to unspool her dreams. What next?

I want time every morning to plan my day without interruptions.

What kind of partner do I want? NOT A USER! Someone who gets excited for my goals. Yes to good listener, able to entertain themselves while I work. Likes to plan fun times. Enjoys my family. Likes to dance!

What makes me *feel* good?

Sophia tapped the pen against her lower lip. That was both an easy question and a difficult one.

Feeling clean, well-groomed, and moisturized. Smelling amazing. Moving my body. Those were the easy answers. The rest were more awkward.

I deeply love my parents, but we are always together. We are all in each other's business, as Cassia puts it. I need to find ways to make some space between us. Idea: Use Cassia's office when she is not living with us. I could even go to the library. Her favorite library was the Biblioteca Angelica, a mere ten-minute walk from her home. The oldest public library in Europe. How could she not dream when surrounded by such beauty and knowledge?

There. That solved that problem, and all she had needed was some alone time to think it up. What was next?

I want enough money to have lovely things. After all, why have plain when you can have fancy?

She doodled a few flowers, filled them in until the page was scattered with purple pansies. As she did that, the ideas began to flow even faster.

I want to remain curious and light-hearted throughout my entire life, like my mother and Nonna, she wrote. *I don't want to be angry and hurtful like Cassia's father or self-absorbed like Emelio. I want to be a positive light and I want other positive lights around me.*

Sophia set down her pen and watched the sun warm up the rose garden. These were beautiful wants and she was already well on her way to making them happen.

Chapter Fourteen

What would you do if you knew you were beautiful?

How to Take Over the World: Affirmations for Glorious Femmes

All that thinking was hungry work. Sophia checked her dual-faced watch. The top face had the time in Rome, the second the time here in Gold Coast. It was just past lunch back home, she noticed, and sent off her first text of the day to her parents.

A beautiful day just dawned here. I'm planning my next moves in my life. How are you all there?

She snapped a photo of the rose garden and sent it, too. She knew her mother especially would enjoy seeing Betsy's roses.

A few moments later, Papa replied. *What did you say to Emelio? He is stomping around, huffing air through his nose like an angry bull.*

Sophia laughed. *I told him that if he wanted my ideas, he had to pay for them.*

Hahahahaahhaah! Mama returned, along with a row of laughing emojis. *Good girl. And what beautiful flowers. I am glad you are taking time to enjoy Gold Coast!*

Her heart warm from the interaction, Sophia packed up her basket. Even though Italian breakfasts were usually a pastry, she felt the urge for something a little more substantial. Time to visit Edna's Diner.

Edna herself waved as Sophia walked into the cute restaurant. The town matriarch leaned against the counter, reading and taking notes from an open book.

"Good morning, lovely Sophia," Edna said, plucking her pen from where it was tucked behind her ear.

"And hello to you, too," Sophia replied. "What are you looking at?"

"I'm expanding my horizons," Edna said. "We've done lots of European foods for our special events here at the diner, but I want to learn more about Asian cooking. This one's on Korean dining. I'm thinking of trying my hand at kimchee."

She pushed the book aside and looked Sophia over. "I know just what you need."

Sophia climbed on top a stool. "What do I need?" she laughed.

"Here." A cold glass of milk slid across the counter. "Everyone needs a little calcium. Now, you drink that, and I'll be right back." Edna disappeared into the kitchen.

Sophia smiled and opened her notebook to a fresh page.

The services I can offer:

- *Hair styling, blow outs, color – including ombre and balayage, recommending hair styles depending on face shape and type of hair, formal event hair.*

- *Clothing styling – able to choose on-trend and classic styles that best flatter a client's figure and lifestyle. I have a strong background in historical and current Italian fashion.*

- *Marketing that doesn't require social media.*

- *Consulting on how to make your job more fun, more profitable, and more enticing for your customers.*

"A breakfast for a hardworking woman." Edna pushed a white plate in front of Sophia. Two poached eggs, the yolks broken, drizzled with lemon and olive oil, were placed on top of toast with basil and avocado. Sautéed butternut squash nestled next to the eggs and toast. "Plenty of protein and veggies for your brain."

"It smells amazing." Sophia sighed. Setting aside her notebook, she tasted the squash. "Delicious."

"It's local," Edna said with an enormous smile. "Hiram grows vegetables in my backyard. He's always trying to come up with something new for the diner."

Sophia chucked. "Like grandmother like grandson, no?"

Edna beamed. "I guess that's true."

The door opened. Dr. Merv, Sheriff Howard, and Webmaster Sal entered, waved at Sophia and Edna, and sat down at the last booth on the left. Edna sauntered over with her pad and the four chatted for a while.

Sophia applied herself to her breakfast, enjoying the murmur of local gossip behind her. Just as she finished up, Cassia and her mother Joan wandered in.

"*Cara,*" Sophia cried out. The two younger women exchanged cheek kisses. Joan gamely leaned in for her greeting, as well.

Cassia nudged Joan. "Go ahead, Mom. Ask her."

Joan bit a fingernail. "Um. You know, what you did for Blanche? The hair?" She gestured vaguely to the top of her head.

Sophia stifled a smile. This was obviously difficult for Joan and giggling wouldn't help. "Yes?"

"I would really like it if you, uh, if you have the time, that is, you know, could do my hair too?" A blotchy flush ran under Joan's pale skin.

"But of course," Sophia answered. "I would be happy to. Do you need breakfast?"

"I don't think I could eat. Can we do it now?" Joan glanced over at the table with the three regulars. Sophia saw Joan's gaze meet Howard's, then she glanced away. The blush deepened and she licked her lips.

Ah. So, some feelings there. "Absolutely." Sophia paid Edna and gathered her belongings. "Let's go. Cassia, will you be joining us?"

Cassia shook her head. "I'll wait until it's all done." She hugged Joan. "Sophia is a genius and will take good care of you."

Sophia couldn't help her own blush at Cassia's praise. In her heart, she knew she was good at what she did, but being ground down by Emelio had left its mark and sometimes she felt doubts creeping in. It was lovely to hear someone praise her.

Why does praise always have to be earned? Why can't it just be something we give each other freely and with joy? Now there was a thought!

"Bye, Edna." Joan threw a glance over her shoulder as they exited the diner, but Sophia noticed that she didn't make eye contact with Edna. She looked at Howard.

Raymond nodded as they entered his barber shop. "Howdy, Joan. You want your nails done, too?"

A slight clicking noise betrayed Joan ripping at her cuticles. "Um...."

"Oh, do," Sophia urged as she ushered Joan into the barber chair. "It will make you feel good."

Joan's glance at Raymond betrayed her nerves. She was afraid of what he would think of her mangled hands, Sophia realized. She flipped the cape over Joan's shoulders. Bending over to fasten the clasps, she whispered, "You lose some of yourself when you worry about how other people see you. Be brave."

Joan swallowed and nodded. Raymond busied himself with gathering the bowls of water and his supplies.

"Now," Sophia said, running her fingers through Joan's hair. "What do you want? What do you like? What would let you know that you are beautiful?"

Joan burst into tears. She pressed her hands over her eyes, but the tears still dripped down her cheeks.

Sophia placed her hands on Joan's shoulders, lightly pressing down.

"I'm so sorry," Joan sobbed. "It feels like all I do is cry."

"Crying is necessary. Healing. Take all the time you need," Sophia soothed.

Finally, Joan swiped at her eyes and lifted her chin. "I want to feel everything I'm not. Beautiful. Smart." A heaving breath. "Sexy. Competent."

"Well, then," Sophia said, exchanging a grin with Raymond. "Let us begin."

"It's a lot of fuss and bother." Joan looked surprised at the words that came out of her mouth. " I'm not worth it."

Chapter Fifteen

What is your fear protecting you from? Is it something you can protect yourself from in a different way? Do you really need that protection at all?

How to Take Over the World: Affirmations for Glorious Femmes

Betsy Whitaker and Lucia de Luca floated in the doorway of Raymond's barber shop. One of the best things about shedding the mortal coil, in Betsy's opinion, was the ability to instantly travel from one place to another. The second-best thing was to meddle in the lives of the living without them ever knowing. Of course, she only ever used her powers for good.

"Oh, dear," Lucia said with a shake of her head and a gentle tut. "The women in this town struggle so much."

Betsy furrowed her brow. "I had hoped that with Alice and Katrina and Cassie getting some freedom, the rest would have followed more easily."

Lucia's gaze was on her granddaughter as Sophia attempted to ease Joan. "It takes what it takes. I know we brought Sophia so she could get over her heartbreak. I didn't know she would have to heal so many others. It is a big job, no?"

"It is," Betsy agreed. "But she's up for it. In my experience, there is no better way to heal the heart than to reach out to others."

"Just as long as she doesn't forget herself in the process," Lucia said firmly.

"She won't. That's why we're here. To remind her."

Betsy's gaze moved to her beloved Raymond. He had been her biggest supporter, her dream-maker. Despite having no interest in the movie industry, he gave her the best feedback on her designs. Then she had died and he had shut down for all these years. He liked to be needed, to help people. She ran her ghostly fingers through his short gray hair.

He froze for a moment, almost as if he could feel her touch. Then, with a shake of his head, he went back to focusing on Joan.

Perhaps he could help young Sophia deal with the crying Joan. It wasn't fair for a young woman, barely twenty-one, to take on the emotional labor of easing Joan's pain.

Raymond saw Sophia shoot him a panicked look. He nodded at her reassuringly.

As Joan sobbed, Raymond got a glass of water and set it on the counter in front of Joan. He sat next to her and clasped her hand between his. Her hands were rough from hard work, the nails nibbled to the quick from nerves. Joan had struggled for years under Eli's behavior. It wouldn't be quick or easy to overcome that pain, but at least she'd made a start. Raymond spoke before Sophia completely freaked out. "That's Eli talking, Joan. That's your lousy dad and those stupid teachers when we went to school."

Sophia's jaw dropped. Raymond sighed. Did she think he didn't notice or care about the people in his town? He rubbed the back of his neck in discomfort. He hadn't, though, had he? He certainly could have done more for Joan and the kids. It was time for him to step up.

"What?" Joan sniffed, glancing up at him.

"You were the best at math in all the school," he grumbled. "And Mister...what was his name? Telling you that girls didn't need to know calculus or science or computers because they would just get married and be farmers' wives."

"Oh, yeah, him. But he was right," Joan said.

Sophia huffed in horror, but otherwise remained quiet.

"He was a sexist jerk." Raymond leaned in closer to Joan. "This town needs your voice, Joanie. You can defy all those men who put you down." He glanced at Sophia. "Betsy taught me that."

A small smile tugged at Sophia's lips, and she gave him a nod. He knew she understood. She'd met Betsy, too. And nobody who ever met Betsy was left unchanged. Even him. Especially him.

Joan stared at him. "You never talk about her."

"Well, maybe I should." He cracked his neck. "Come on. Your hair isn't going to cut itself."

Sophia was relieved when Joan finally relaxed and allowed Sophia to wash her hair. Back on familiar ground, she was able to see that Joan needed roses all around. She poured the rose water she'd made with Blanche through Joan's wet tresses, then put some cotton balls soaked in the hydrosol on Joan's swollen eyes.

"Oh, that feels good." Joan almost melted into the chair.

Raymond, massaging her hands, said, "Give yourself permission to do things that make yourself feel good, Joan. It's the secret to success."

Sophia met his gaze. The familiar words resonated deep in her soul. It matched up with everything she'd decided she wanted for her life. To make others feel good. To make herself feel good. "My Nonna Lucia used to say that."

"I think she's where Betsy learned it," Raymond said. "She always said that she did her best work when she felt joyous and supported."

"I haven't felt that way in a long time," Joan sighed.

"Then it is time to find your sisterhood." Sophia leaned Joan upright and nabbed her scissors. "Let us see if we can make you see in yourself what we see in you."

An hour and a half later, Sophia asked, "Are you ready to see yourself?"

"Yes," Joan murmured. "Oh, yes."

Sophia spun the chair and Joan gasped. "Is that me?"

Sophia grinned at Joan's reflection. Her straight, gray hair fell in a long, smooth sweep to her shoulder blades. A center part drew attention to her still-dark eyebrows and bright eyes. A little product gave body, lift, and shine so the strands shone like pewter. Again, Sophia had dusted Joan's skin with some gold shimmer, bringing warmth to her face.

She stood, leaning even closer to the mirror. "It's like I've never seen myself before." Her now-elegant fingers ran through her sweet-smelling hair, trailed over her newly smooth facial skin. "I can't believe it. I'm reborn," Joan murmured. Her reflected gaze met Sophia's, then Raymond's. "Thank you, you two. Thank you. Thank you so much."

Raymond pinned a purple rose behind her ear. "Are you ready to be seen, Joan?"

"Yes. Oh, yes!" This time when her eyes welled with tears, Sophia knew it was because Joan was happy. Wishing to prolong the moment, she asked, "Would you like some lessons in how to take care of your hair and skin?"

Joan beamed. "That would be helpful, thank you. It's been a long time since I even thought about taking care of myself."

By the time Joan left the barbershop, she had a bag full of scent, lotions, toner, and cleanser. "I love all these." She grinned.

"Now go forth and amaze yourself," Sophia cheered as Joan exited the barber shop.

Raymond held his fist out. She bumped it with her own.

Happiness flooded her. *This* was what she was meant to do.

Chapter Sixteen

Let go of those things that drain your energy, your joy, your soul.
How to Take Over the World: Affirmations for Glorious Femmes

J oan carefully shut the barbershop door behind her and stood there for a moment, trying to gather herself together. She felt a thousand pounds lighter and a thousand watts brighter. She felt like marching down the street, waving like a beauty queen, but at the same time ducking her head so no one could see, embarrassed that she'd spent time and money on herself.

She realized that was her old self talking, though. The part that Eli had pounded into the dirt with his cruel words. She'd spent so much time embarrassed by Eli and ashamed of herself that she'd constantly existed in a state of shame.

Shame.

She tilted her head up. As much as it hurt to admit, she had failed her children by not leaving Eli. The boys still acted out. Her daughter was cautious around her. Her lower lip wobbled. She stiffened her spine. That was in the past. From this moment on, she was going to live in a different way. She would put those things behind her and start again. This was her new life, and she was going to live it to the fullest. Or at least she was going to try.

She stepped onto the sidewalk and started down the street when a voice behind her said, "Joany?"

She turned and it felt like her heart leapt out of her chest. Her cheeks flushed and her pulse raced. "Oh, hello, Howard. How are you?"

He gave her that lopsided grin he used to give her back in high school. The same one that made her fall— Well, that was in the past. She'd been young and silly and read too much into Howard's kindness.

"I'm doing just fine, Joany. How about yourself? You look really pretty." He tucked his thumbs in his belt loops and leaned back on his heels. His uniform was neatly pressed, and his badge was polished until it gleamed.

Her cheeks heated and she almost ducked her head again, but at the last minute she managed not to. Instead, she gripped the strap of her purse tightly and politely said, "Thank you, Howard. That's very kind of you. I'm doing alright. What are you doing today?"

Howard nodded toward The Café of Hopes and Dreams. "Taking a break. Thought I'd grab a cup of coffee."

"Oh, you're working then." She winced. Of course, he was working. He was in his uniform, for goodness' sake. *Stupid, Joan. Why do you have to say something so stupid?*

But Howard didn't act like what she'd said was stupid. Instead, he gave her another smile that made her heart flutter and reminded her of the boy he'd been. He'd gone gray now and was softer around the middle than he'd once been, but he was still the handsomest man in the whole of Gold Coast as far as she was concerned.

"Yep. Long day today. Dorrie called in sick, so doing a double shift." Dorrie was one of the part-time deputies.

"Oh, well, I'm sorry about that," Joan said, not sure what else to say.

She was about to make excuses and head home when Howard said, "Join me for a cup of coffee?"

She blinked. Had he just asked her to coffee? Her stomach fluttered. "Um—sure. Yeah, I guess that'd be fine." After all, she'd just told Raymond that she was ready to be seen. If that meant being seen by Howard, even better.

He beamed. "Great. Right this way." He ushered her into the café, his touch light and firm on her shoulder, like they were on a date or something.

Don't read anything into it, Joan. It's just coffee. He's being friendly. He doesn't mean anything by it.

"What'll it be?" Howard said, eyeing the menu behind the counter.

"Oh, just regular coffee will do."

He snorted. "Come on, Joany, live a little. Don't you have something to celebrate?"

She mulled it over. She did have a new look, that was something to celebrate, right? A new look, a new start on life. She found herself grinning. "I guess I do. I'll have a Viennese mocha." It sounded fancy and she kind of liked the idea of something fancy.

"Would you like a slice of Sacher torte? It goes really well with the Viennese mocha," Katrina said. "Marie says it's too much chocolate, but I say there's no such thing."

"Sure," Joan found herself saying. She hadn't meant to say yes, but it had just kind of come out.

"And I'll have a vanilla latte with a slice of your honeycomb cake," Howard said, pulling out his wallet. When Joan went to protest, he held up his hand. "My treat."

She wanted to protest again. She didn't like to impose. But then he had invited her, right? Why shouldn't she accept? They were old school mates, right? And if he insisted on paying, well, that was just him being nice. There was nothing more to it. It was no different than having a bite with Sophia or Alice or Edna.

The problem was, she'd had a crush on Howard since her freshman year in high school. It was unrequited, of course, and she'd never let him know, but she'd watched him from afar, her heart fluttering every time he looked her way or crooked that lazy grin of his. He'd been so handsome. She was sure he hadn't even known she was alive. Well, he knew her, of course, because this was a small town, but he didn't really register her. But she'd done all the silly things teenage girls did like collect little mementos and write his name in her notebook. Eli had thrown away her yearbooks, but senior year, Joan had bought a photograph of him from the annual photo sale. She had managed to nab a flower that had fallen from his boutonniere flower. The picture and the tiny dried spray of baby's breath had survived Eli's purge since she had hidden them in with her feminine products..

High school was a long time ago. They were both adults. He simply had no idea that a tiny little part of her was still that teenaged girl.

She hid it all through the years of her marriage to Eli, as a sweet memento of her crush. When she'd had dreams of Howard bending her over his muscled arm and kissing her until her head spun. That would have been just the beginning of an adventurous life together.

But that was just a fantasy, a childish one, and it was all in the past. They had long gone their separate ways, made their choices. Those dreams were never meant to be, so she set them firmly aside.

Howard led them to a table with a good view of Main Street. He even pulled out her chair for her. He was so gentlemanly and kind. It made her feel like a queen. First her new look and now this? She'd better be careful it didn't go to her head.

She froze. That was Eli talking. Why shouldn't she let it "go to her head"? Everyone deserved to be treated well and to treat themselves well, right?

She smiled as Howard took the seat across from her. It had been a long time since she simply sat and had a conversation with a friend and enjoyed the afternoon. How did one even start? Perhaps with something simple. "So I hear Leilani's goat went on the lam again."

Howard chuckled, his eyes sparkling. "Pretty sure that's why Dorrie called in sick today. She's been chasing that goat for three days and still hasn't caught him."

Joan felt her shoulders relax as she let go of her worries and simply enjoyed the moment.

Sophia carefully cleaned her station, humming along to the tune on the old radio. Something peppy and fun. She placed her scissors and combs and clips into a large jar filled with blue disinfectant. The harsh fumes from the liquid stung her nose, but Raymond had assured her it would get the job done.

"We make a good team." Raymond kept his eyes on his sweeping, but his words seemed to curl softly through the air, barely louder than the music.

"We do," she agreed. "I really appreciate your help with Joan today. I had no idea what to say." It hurt to admit that. She'd always felt like she was in control when she wielded her scissors. As if divine wisdom flowed from the blades into her so she could impart it to her client. But with Joan Mack, she'd floundered. The woman's pain and grief and loneliness had been overwhelming and completely beyond her ability to address.

"Joany's had a hard life," Raymond said softly as he dumped the final bits from the dustpan into the garbage. He tucked the broom and dustpan away in the corner. "A lot of folks around here have, of course, but she's had it worse than most. Her husband—well, almost ex-husband, I suppose he is now—was not a good man."

"Cassia has told me a bit about that," Sophia said. It had made her so grateful that her own father, Leo, was so wonderful and warm. She could never imagine him speaking to her or her mother in such an awful way as Cassia's father had. She was glad Eli Mack was in jail and couldn't hurt his family anymore.

"Cassie and Joany suffered a great deal," Raymond said, jaw working. "But things are better now. They're healing. Growing stronger. We just have to make sure they stay safe so they can keep healing and growing." He straightened his shoulders as if determined to stand guard against any and all who would harm the Mack women.

Sophia hid a smile. Raymond had never struck her as the chivalrous type, but clearly deep inside was a knight in shining armor just waiting to get out. "Yes, you are right. That is exactly what we must do."

And not just for Cassia and Joan Mack, but for all the women in Gold Coast. Women like her new friend Blanche, who had lost herself and her power because of a husband who smothered her. Who was only now sprouting fragile tendrils of hope and joy. Tendrils that could get easily crushed. They all needed encouragement to grow, to rediscover their own strength, and Sophia knew she was meant to help.

The question was, how?

Chapter Seventeen

Knowledge of the past reveals a better future.

How to Take Over the World: Affirmations for Glorious Femmes

Early in the morning, Sophia typed *most popular body care scents* into the search bar of her browser and studied the results. She and Blanche could make their own peppermint, lemon, and lavender essential oils. Rose, too, if she could convince Raymond to give her his harvest. Bergamot, though, looked complicated to produce and would be best sourced from a commercial producer. She jotted some notes, preparing for her next meeting with Blanche.

"Sophia?" Cassia called up the stairs to their apartment over The Café of Hopes and Dreams.

Sophia lifted her fingers from her laptop. "Yes?" she shouted back.

"You need to come down here." Cassia's voice sounded strained.

What could have possibly gone wrong that Cassia and Katrina couldn't handle? She saved her document and hurried down to the bakery.

"What is it, darling?" she asked Cassia as she stepped into the kitchen, the warm scent of baking scones making her stomach rumble.

Her friend tipped her head toward a table. Her face was strangely flushed, and her eyes sparked almost angrily.

Confused by Cassie's reaction, Sophia glanced at the table she'd indicated. Her body froze and she felt like her legs might give out any moment.

"*Buongiorno*, my love." Emelio Greco, perfectly groomed and in a partially structured pale peach sport coat, stood up from his chair. In his hand was an enormous bouquet of roses and oleanders.

"B-but how are you here?" she blurted. This was the last place in the entire world she'd expected to see him.

"I have come to win you back," he said in Italian.

Sophia's stomach sank to her feet. Her heart pounded triple time. A bead of sweat dripped down her back, tickling her spine. Of all the things that could have happened to her, this was the very last thing she would have thought of.

Was she numb? Was she excited? Was she happy to see him? Sophia had no idea. Her mind blanked. He stepped forward, put the flowers in her hands, and kissed her cheeks more tenderly than he ever had.

"I've made a mistake. I didn't realize you were the light of my heart until you told me you would charge me for your ideas. Then, boom!" He gestured with his fingers, miming an explosion. "I knew I was wrong. That you were everything to me. I asked my sister to run the restaurant, but I only have three days here. Let me show you I have changed." He pushed the bunch into her hands.

"Ah, thank you," she said automatically. Sophia held the flowers, the thorns pricking her fingers. Red and pink roses mixed in with the creamy white oleanders. Automatically, she smelled the bouquet, a dim part of her mind realizing they had been cut from the Betsy Whitaker Memorial Garden just moments ago, the dew still on the petals.

He remembered. He remembered that once she had asked for roses fresh with dew. He laughed back then. Maybe he really had changed. She frowned a little. Or did he think she would take him back just because he remembered one thing about her?

He wasn't laughing now, though. His brown eyes were warm with appreciation. "You look lovely," he commented, gazing at her lips.

His compliments had always made her stomach clench. They still did. She smoothed her hair with her free hand. Her mouth felt dry. His kisses could be so sweet, she remembered, his touch firm. "Thank you, again." She dropped her hand, angry at her lapse. No, no, no. No more of his games.

She took a step back, placing the flowers on the table. He'd hurt her badly with his behavior. He'd taken advantage of her, used her, tried to destroy her family's business, and now he just showed up, stole some flowers, and peppered her with compliments and thought it would all be better? "What do you want, Emelio? I cannot believe you traveled across the world just to speak with me. You could have emailed."

"But then I could not have seen your face." He pulled a set of keys out of his front pocket, a charging bull on the sleek metal tag. "Let me take you for drive, mia amata," he purred.

"I especially rented a Lamborghini for you. You did say you wanted to experience a luxury car. With your permission, I'll drive you to the stars, gioia mia. "

Her jaw dropped. She'd said that once when she was a little tipsy, talking about their bucket lists, dreams they had of wealth and abundance. She'd meant something more like the American Cadillac or a Mercedes, something plush and smooth and silent that would take them to the north of Italy in comfort. But a Lamborghini? Sure, she was curious about such a famous vehicle, but this was excessive.

"Um," she delayed. Everything about this was too much. His unexpected appearance, his grand gesture with the expensive car. How much did those cost? What should she do? She had never anticipated that he would act like this.

"What do you say?" he coaxed. "Just a little drive won't hurt anyone."

She rubbed her collarbone. "Emelio, I just don't think—"

"My heart. It's okay to stop thinking and enjoy something. I know how you work and think all the time. Let me give you some fun."

She glanced at Cassia. Cassia was watching Emelio as if he were a batch of bread she wasn't sure would rise properly. Her gaze drifted back to Sophia. "Come help me pack some food for your trip," she said.

"Take your time." Emelio sat back down and sipped his espresso.

When they reached the back kitchen, Sophia stared at Cassia in confusion. "Why are you encouraging me to do this?"

"Look," she said, "the sooner you find out what he really wants, the sooner you will get rid of him. Besides, this is the honeymoon phase where he's gonna woo you like some kind of prince. Might as well enjoy it a little, huh?" Cassie winked.

"What if he's pushy?" She clasped her hands together, trying to regain control of the situation.

Cassia grinned. "That's why I texted Howard. He'll be tailing you." She handed over a box of baked goods. "Now. Go enjoy your ride."

"Very well. Thank you." Sophia nodded. She ran upstairs, grabbed her purse, and met Emelio in the café.

He gave her his smoothest smile. A little curl of anger lit in her belly. How dare he try to manipulate her like this?

"I will take us across this long state, and we will watch the sun set over the Mississippi River," he promised effusively.

She exchanged glances with Cassia, then looked back at Emelio. "Perfect," she said dryly.

After Sophia and Emelio exited the café, Katrina tapped her nails on the top of the glass display case, imitating a drum roll. "I don't like that Emelio thinks getting Sophia back will be easy."

"Or worse, that she might fall for his nonsense," Cassie agreed.

"I think we need to put a few more obstacles in his way." Katrina pulled her phone from her apron pocket.

Within twenty minutes, every woman in Gold Coast who wanted to meet Sophia agreed to visit during the next two days. Cassie nodded. "If he handles her being the center of attention, then we know he's really changed."

"But if he gets pouty, we will know exactly what his game is." Katrina smirked.

It felt like half the town clustered around the low-slung wedge shape of Emelio's car. Sal bent over, peering into the interior. Howard stood behind it, his arms crossed, and his eyes narrowed. Raymond lovingly stroked the bright yellow hood. Alice and Henry stood in the doorway of their store, eyes wide. Edna had plunked herself in front of the driver's door, blocking Emelio's way.

"You," she pointed at him, "will be a safe driver and bring our girl home in one piece, with no tickets."

Emelio laughed. "Of course, mio graziosa signora."

Edna snorted, completely unaffected by his charm. She moved to one side, still glaring.

Sophia smiled at her protector. "I will be fine," she said, opening the passenger door. "I've always wanted to do something like this."

Once inside the car, Sophia tied an ice-blue scarf around her hair as Emelio lowered the roof of the Lamborghini. He winked at her and, with a casual flick of his wrist, unsnapped his sunglasses. He looked like the magazine ideal of the Italian man: handsome, with a light stubble and wearing his clothes with that special confidence called sprezzatura. Knowing he wanted a reaction, she fanned herself dramatically. Perhaps she could use his fashionable example to help the gentlemen of Gold Coast experiment with new things. Like jewelry. And color. And clothes that fit. He started the car. The precision-tuned engine started off with a low rumble that made her catch her breath. Emelio grinned wildly and stomped on the accelerator. The rumble shifted into a low scream, like a giant cat proclaiming its superiority, like fine silk velvet tearing under a passionate lover.

The vibrations spread throughout her body, making her tender skin quiver. Oh, this was better than she'd even imagined a fine Italian luxury car would be.

She flicked her gaze quickly toward Emelio and back before he caught her looking. She couldn't help but wish that *she* was the one in the driver's seat, hands on the steering wheel.

Emelio peeled out in a plume of dark smoke. She wrinkled her nose, glad when they left the scent of burnt rubber behind. She wasn't surprised that Emelio felt the need to show off, but it was...disappointing.

He still performed best with an audience.

Howard and the rest of the men stood in the street, watching the taillights disappear.

"What a jerk," Sal said with a shake of his head.

"Someone's insecure," Raymond commented.

Henry snorted.

Howard jingled his keys in his pocket and smiled. "Time for me to follow along."

Chapter Eighteen

*We need style **and** substance for a wonderful life.*

How to Take Over the World: Affirmations for Glorious Femmes

The Lamborghini howled against the pavement as Emelio downshifted through the Shawnee National Forest. The tires squealed with each turn as he pressed the accelerator harder, taking turns faster than the posted safety limit. They were going at least thirty miles faster than the speed limit, and Sophia was sure that any moment they would veer off the road or get pulled over by the police. This was not the lovely drive in the countryside that she'd envisioned.

She did love the beautiful car, the rumble of the powerful engine, the feel of the road beneath her. But she didn't love the recklessness with which Emelio drove. She didn't feel...safe.

"Could you slow down? We can't really see the landscape," she asked.

"Let go, beautiful," he cooed, not taking his foot off the accelerator. "You don't have to be in control all the time." With that, he pressed the pedal harder.

Her hand tightened on the door handle until the skin on her knuckles turned white and her joints ached. As the trees and hills whipped by too fast to observe, she realized that she never had felt safe with Emelio.

Not since the early days when they were first wrapped in the cocoon of love, and everything was beautiful and rosy. Back then she hadn't considered feeling safe as an important thing. In fact, she hadn't thought of it one way or the other. She loved him and he loved her and that was all in the world that mattered.

When he'd taken her first idea to spruce up his family's restaurant, she'd been delighted. Even when he'd told his father the idea was his, she'd brushed any negative thoughts aside and instead focused on the thrill that he'd used *her* idea.

Was that it? Was that the moment she'd lost the feeling of being safe with him? Oh, he was still sexy and fun and exciting, but perhaps she'd trusted him a little less.

Or was it the day she'd caught him flirting with Alessia Bianchi from the shop across the way. He'd claimed he was just "networking," but she'd seen the way he'd touched Alessia's hand and stroked her arm. It was not a "networking" sort of touch. It was the touch of a man persuading a lover. And while Sophia had brushed it aside and accepted his word, a little part of her had stopped trusting him quite as much as before.

The car lurched a little as Emelio took a turn too quickly and Sophia clenched the door handle harder, a shiver of panic working itself though her. This was a lot less fun than she or Cassie had thought. This was not the kind of adventure she wanted. Experiences, yes. Things that made her fear for her life? No.

They hit a straight stretch and Emelio glanced in the rearview mirror and muttered a curse.

"What is it?" She glanced behind to see a police vehicle, its lights swirling. Her heart lurched. But as Emelio slowed the car, she felt herself settle, oddly glad they were being stopped. She closed her eyes, willing herself to breathe.

Finally, the car stopped, and Emelio rolled the window down, scowling at the uniformed officer who appeared. The man leaned down, and Sophia couldn't help a small gasp.

"Afternoon, folks," Howard drawled. "Do you know why I pulled you over?"

Emelio's scowl grew darker. "Because you're jealous?"

Sophia pressed her hand to her mouth, but Howard just chuckled.

"You were going thirty miles over the posted speed limit," he said, unfazed by the rage pulsing off Emelio. "Going to have to write you a ticket." Howard scribbled something on the pad in his hand. "License and registration, please."

"This is ridiculous," Emelio snarled through thin-pressed lips as he forked over his ID.

"Well, looks like you're from out of the country. You're going to have to pay this ticket before you leave town." Howard said calmly.

Emelio glanced at Sophia and suddenly a smile broke across his face, replacing the angry scowl. "Of course, of course. I will definitely do that. You are right, of course, I was speeding. I apologize, sir."

Howard handed back Emelio's paperwork along with a yellow ticket. "You can come by the station anytime during your visit to pay the fine."

"Yes, yes. Of course." Emelio beamed widely as if he'd been given a prize, but Sophia hadn't forgotten his nasty slip of temper.

"Enjoy your drive, just keep it under the speed limit." Howard tipped his hat and strolled back to his squad car.

As he pulled back onto the blacktop, Emelio's smile was firmly in place, but the muscles in his jaw flexed. Sophia expected him to rant once they were back on the road, but he didn't. This was improvement, she thought. He was angry, but he wasn't turning that anger onto her.

After a few more minutes, he pulled onto a scenic overlook off the highway and turned off the engine. He got out and dashed around the car to open her door.

"What are we doing here, Emelio?"

"It's such a lovely day and I am with such a lovely woman. I think we should enjoy the view." He gestured expansively, then offered his hand like in the movies.

She let him help her from the car and stood with him next to the railing, overlooking a creek with a small step waterfall. The gentle cascade of water from one step to another blended with the call of birds and made for lovely backdrop music. The leaves of the trees were shades of gold and orange and vibrant red as late summer blended into fall. It was such a peaceful, beautiful place. She almost couldn't believe Emelio had thought to bring her here. It reminded her of their early days together when they had picnics in the Villa Borghese, the most famous park in all of Rome. They would spend hours there, enjoying each other and not even noticing the view, although the park was a splendid work of natural art.

"This is so pretty," she said, leaning her elbows on the rail. "How did you know to come here?"

He shrugged. "I did a little research. I wanted to find somewhere we could enjoy nature together as we used to." His voice turned low and sweet, and she felt her insides flutter.

This was the Emelio she remembered. The one who was caring and thoughtful and wanted to please her and make her happy. "I love it."

"You are the love of my life, Sophia. I can't live without you. And I'm going to win you back."

Chapter Nineteen

Who are the members of your sisterhood?

How to Take Over the World: Affirmations for Glorious Femmes

Cassie watched with narrowed eyes as the bright yellow Lamborghini whipped back into town. Honestly, she thought it was the ugliest car she'd ever seen. She preferred vintage cars with curvy lines and fishtails and things like that. Give her a powder blue '57 Chevy any day.

Emelio jumped out of the car, raced around the side, and helped Sophia out like she was a princess. Cassie didn't buy the act. Not for one second. Maybe she was overly suspicious, but she'd seen how Emelio had treated Sophia when they were in

Rome. Those horrible, awful things he'd said to her. The look of disgust on his face when he looked at Cassie's friend. Nope, she didn't buy that he'd changed that much.

Once a snake, always a snake.

She crossed her arms and watched through the front window of the café as Emelio offered his arm gallantly and Sophia took it. How could she stand to be near that...worm?

Of course, Cassie was familiar with abusive men. Her father, Eli, had been much the same toward her mother. He'd say nasty things all day long, demanding she cater to his whims and clean up after him. Then it was like Eli knew when Joan was on the verge of being done with him. Of maybe walking out. Suddenly, he'd change and toss her a few compliments, say nice things about her cooking, shower her with attention, or a small gift like a flower he'd plucked from someone else's yard. Once Joan was back under his spell—Cassie had no other explanation for it—Eli would go back to his old ways, yelling at her and calling her names.

Cassie suspected Emelio was cut from the same cloth as Eli Mack. There was no way he could keep up with this for long. He'd show his true colors soon enough. And she was going to help him along.

She sent Edna a quick text: *They're back. Phase 1 commencing.*

"Okay, Katrina, we're on," she said out loud.

Katrina, who was behind the counter, let out a chuckle. "Good luck."

With a smile, Cassie tucked her phone in her back pocket and dashed out the door of the café. She powerwalked up the sidewalk until she was right behind the two lovebirds.

Ew. Just the thought of it made her queasy.

"Sophia!" she shouted.

The two whirled to face her. A look of concern crossed Sophia's face, but Emelio's eyes narrowed before he could hide it. Cassie tamped down the smug feeling of being right. Now was not the time. She had a mission to fulfill!

"Cassia, is everything alright?" Sophia's brow creased.

"I need your help. Hurry. It's important." She grabbed Sophia's hand and pulled her back toward the café.

Sophia came along willingly while Emelio spluttered behind them, obviously not at all happy about his little plan getting usurped. Too bad.

Cassie pulled her friend inside the café and shoved her into one of the chairs. "Stay here. I'll be right back."

Ignoring Emelio's protests, Cassie dashed into the kitchen where Katrina had a plate ready. With a grin, she pushed the plate at Cassie who grabbed it and strode back to the table. She placed the plate in front of Sophia and plopped into the chair across from her, leaving Emelio no place to sit at the small, two-person bistro table.

"Macarons?" Sophia stared down at the colorful little cookies sitting in front of her.

"Yes. I have made two of each flavor, French and Italian. I need to know which style you prefer."

"This is an emergency?" Emelio said. "All this for stupid macarons?" His face grew red as he glared at Cassie. "You little..."

Sophia glanced up at Emelio, eyes wide.

Cassie kept her expression calm, but inside she was practically giddy. This was it. He was going to show his true colors.

Instead, he took a deep breath and seemed to wrangle himself under control. A bland smile crossed his lips. "It's good that you trust my Sophia's opinion. She is fond of her pastries."

To anyone else, it sounded like a compliment, but Cassie was well aware of the hidden barb. She thought Sophia was, too, by the look on her face, but then she could tell the minute Sophia brushed it off.

"Why don't you join me in the taste test, Emelio?" Sophia said softly. "I'm sure Cassia would love your opinion, too."

Cassie most definitely wouldn't, but there wasn't much she could do, so she got up and waved at her vacated seat. While Emelio turned on the charm, she sent Edna another text: *Phase 1 failure* □.

Edna quickly texted back: *Do not give up, Cassie. Phase 2 will commence soon.*

Cassie stared at the back of Emelio's head. *Just you wait, Mr. Snake. We've got your number. You don't fool us.*

And hopefully, he soon wouldn't be able to fool Sophia anymore either.

Phase 2 now go, she texted the rest of the town.

Chapter Twenty

It takes a team to take over the world.

How to Take Over the World: Affirmations for Glorious Femmes

Cheryl Parker and Pamela Collins had been best friends since pre-school. Since before they were out of diapers, they had been inseparable. So no one along Main Street noticed when they strode, side-by-side, out Books and Bait and past the gas station. Years of being in marching band had increased their tendencies to walk in step.

Betsy Whittaker and Lucia de Luca floated behind them, smiling at the two high school juniors.

"I do believe they will do well," Betsy commented. "They picked right up on our hints."

"I think they figured it out when you forced their electronic issue of *Teen Vogue* to only show ads for skin and hair care." Lucia snorted.

"They were there for the fashion show," Betsy said. "They saw what Sophia can do. They just needed a little push."

"And we need to test Emelio before my darling girl decides on him," Lucia growled.

The two ghosts turned their heads when a classic ice cream truck, hot pink tropical flowers painted over the original white body, took the corner of First Street and Main a little fast, then parked, facing the wrong way, in front of the new farmer's market shop.

"Hey, isn't that Leilani Jones?" Cheryl asked.

"Yeah. I wonder what she is doing in town." Pamela scratched her face, then pulled her hand away. Angry red pimples crossed her jawline up to her temple.

"I heard there might be a market in town," Cheryl replied. "Maybe they would like some of your mosaics?"

Pamela grunted. "Unlikely." She flipped her braid over her shoulder, trying to take some of weight of her heavy hair off her neck.

Lucia and Betsy exchanged a long, sad look at Pamela's defeated tone. The girl was from a long line of practical people who saw no value in her creativity. Only her best friend, Cheryl, seemed interested in cheering on her endeavors. Unfortunately, Pamela was at a crossroads. If she allowed herself to be steered down the practical path...well, neither ghost was about to let that happen if they could help it.

Leliani, with her long black hair covered by a green knitted beanie, pulled a wheeled cooler full of rattling bottles into the store.

"She's here," Pamela breathed, her gaze zeroed in on Sophia's figure silhouetted in the shop's front window.

"Look at her. I don't know if I hate her or want to be her," Cheryl muttered. Her dirty-dishwater brown hair hung limply on her head, and she touched it a little self-consciously.

Inside the future farmer's market, the lovely Italian girl spoke quickly to a handsome man in a soft-looking, black and grey checked sport coat.

"And look at him," Cheryl continued. "Why don't we have anyone who looks like that here?"

They both sighed at his well-groomed hair and polished shoes. Nope. Definitely no men like that in Gold Coast.

"Well, we aren't getting any younger out here." Pamela, unconsciously quoting her mother, nodded her head firmly. "Let's go ask her."

Leliani and Missus Sandersen were in the corner by a glass fronted refrigerator, talking excitedly about dairy products. The two Italians stood furthest from those two, the man whispering in an impassioned voice.

The girls paused in the doorway, frozen with the enormity of what they wanted.

Betsy and Lucia exchanged glances. The girls couldn't hear him, but as ghosts, they could hear everything Emelio said.

"Sophia, it is time to come home. You have done all you can do in this tiny place. Come back to Rome, where you belong. With me."

"Go on, young ones," Betsy urged in the teenagers' ears.

"Now is the time to interrupt him." Lucia grinned, thrilled with their plotting.

The teenagers didn't move.

"Dammit." Betsy pinched the bridge of her nose and wrinkled her brow. Pamela's cell phone played the *Wonder Woman* theme.

"Who could this be?" she muttered and pulled her phone out of her backpack. "*Don't waste your time. Make the changes you need now*," she read out loud.

"Who sent that?" Cheryl rubbed the back of her neck.

"Unknown number. Weird." Pamela shrugged. "Well, whoever they are, they are right." With that, they both firmed their jaws and stepped into the store.

Sophia turned away from the handsome man, a sudden smile lighting up her face. "Hello. How can I help you?"

"Um." Pamela shoved her hands in her jeans' pockets. "We saw you at the fashion show."

"Can you make us look like you?" Cheryl blurted out.

Emelio gave the two a once-over, a sneer turning his handsome features ugly. His opinion of them was both obvious and unkind.

Oblivious to Emelio's reaction, Sophia's eyes widened. "Better yet. I can make you look like *you*." She patted Emelio's shoulder and led them out the shop door and across the street to the barber shop.

Emelio stood, gaping like a well-groomed fish.

Lucia and Betsy made fists and knuckle-bumped each other. "Phase Three begun!" Lucia laughed.

Three hours later, Pamela walked out of the barber shop. Her dark, waist-length hair had been cut and styled into a charming 1920's bob, making her eyes look large and luminous. The redness and the inflammation on her jawline had been eased. But most of all she now walked with her head up, shoulders back, as if she were ready to take on the world. She carried a bag with a facial cleanser and a gentle skin toner, both of which would make her feel special and pampered.

"Remember that actress from the black and white films?" Lucia asked.

"Louise Brooks?" Betsy guessed.

"Yeah. She looks her. Very classy."

Betsy agreed. Pamela had blossomed under Sophia's hands.

Cheryl followed her friend out onto the sidewalk. Her hair had been cut shorter and gelled into punk-rock spikes. The style highlighted her high cheekbones and elfin features, and she grinned as if she simply couldn't stop smiling at the world, the happiness and joy inside her bursting to get out. Her bag was full to bursting of Sophia's goodies.

"Your granddaughter has an amazing gift," Betsy remarked.

"I'm very proud of her." Lucia dabbed her eyes. "She is incredible. This town of yours woke her up. And it's about time."

Best of all, Emelio had given up and was nowhere to be seen. Although Betsy had the unfortunate feeling he was lurking somewhere nearby, waiting for his next moment.

As if reading her mind Lucia said, "We must remain vigilant. That boy is like a snake in the grass, waiting to strike."

"Indeed, we must."

If Emelio was a snake, then she and Lucia would be the mongoose.

Chapter Twenty-One

What is your pain? How can you ease it?

How to Take Over the World: Affirmations for Glorious Femmes

Alice Kennedy pursed her lips. Across the street Emelio sat next to Sophia at the little sidewalk table in front of The Cafe, lifting a green macaron to her lips. That must have been the pistachio one that Cassie had worried about. A red cookie sat on a plate in front of Sophia, obviously a raspberry.

The minute Cheryl and Pamela had cleared the shop, Emelio had been all over Sophia, urging her to join him for desserts from the café. Now he gazed lovingly into her eyes as she nibbled on the difficult-to-make macarons. He leaned over and licked a crumb from her lips. Sophia's eyes fluttered shut and she lifted her face to his.

Nope, nope, nope. Alice wasn't about to let the coolest chick she knew fall back in love with that user.

"Hey, Sophia," Alice shouted across the street.

Emelio jerked back from his kiss.

"Yes, Alice?" Sophia answered. It was hard to tell if she was disappointed or relieved by the interruption.

"I need your suggestions. I'm trying to figure out the theme for The Thing next year and I am completely stuck." Shoot. That didn't sound urgent. "I have to get the design ready because of advertising."

"Oh, of course, Alice." Sophia pushed away from the little table.

"But Sophia," Emelio captured her hand and lifted it to his lips. "I did come here for you. Please don't interrupt our time together again. Isn't that what you were always saying, that we didn't have enough calm time between us?"

Sophia gestured at Alice. "You and I will have the rest of our lives to have calm time. I'll only be in Gold Coast for a little while longer."

Alice winced at the "rest of our lives" comment. Surely Sophia wasn't planning to marry this joker? This was worse than she thought!

He rested Sophia's hand against his cheek. "*Carissima.* You know I love your impulsiveness and generosity. I want you to aim that at me, at keeping us together."

Alice resisted the urge to gag. Henry would never say such a thing to her. He liked that she had friends, that she had ambition and talents, just as he did. Everything they did apart added to the sparkle of their time together. They never ran out of interesting things to talk about, because they were both doing interesting things.

Her heart warmed at her affection for Henry, and she could feel the dumb smile on her face that she always got when she thought of him. *Never mind,* she told herself. She was here to keep Emelio Greco from love bombing Sophia.

"Please don't ignore me while I've gone to so much trouble to be here." He kissed the inside of Sophia's wrist, subtly yanking her back toward the table.

Alice winced. He had a point. He had gone to a great deal of expense and hassle to travel at the last minute, rent a fancy car, to admit he was wrong. Not that she bought that last part for a hot minute. It was all a ploy. She was pretty sure Emelio didn't have a sincere bone in his body. He only did all those things to look good to Sophia, not because he meant them.

What to do?

Flattery, of course.

She waved her arm to regain their attention. "Of course, I mean you too, Emelio," she said, her voice carrying. "I need your excellent taste and knowledgeable eyes for these projects." She was well aware it was Sophia who had the taste while Emelio took the credit.

His eyebrows lifted at her, casting a suspicious look her way. "Is that so."

"The first Thing was a Venice Carnivale theme. The next one needs to be even better, but I'm running out of ideas. I know you live with amazing design. Any ideas you two have would really level this up further."

The two Romans glanced at each other. Sophia nodded. "It will be fun," she coaxed, pulling at Emelio's hand that was still clasping hers.

Eventually, he nodded back, reclaiming his hand and pushing up from the table. "Very well. *Obviously*, you need help."

Emelio held out his hand to help Sophia up. She took the assistance and then dropped his grasp when she started across the street. Alice bit her lip to hide a smile. Perhaps Sophia wasn't as besotted as Gold Coast worried.

She held the door open to The Dream Factory. Sophia glided in, her pupils dilated and her shoulders back. Emelio followed, his eyebrows furrowed and his lips tight in what had to be suspicion.

He studied the sewing studio she had set up in one of the front windows, his gaze captured by the colorful rows of thread on one wall and the dressmaker's dummy clad in a long, red kimono in the other window. The pictures and play script next to the kimono informed the viewer that these costumes were being made for a Kabuki production of *Titus Andronicus* for the University of Illinois at Edwardsville.

His eyebrows lifted in surprise and the color rose in his cheeks "That is beautiful." His tone indicated he was surprised by the quality of her work. He inspected the seams, his fingers running down each stitch. He smoothed the fabric. "I really like how you lined up all the legs for this octopus. Perfect job. Where did you find this pattern?"

"Thank you. I found it online from a New York fabric house," Alice replied, surprised by his compliments. "I really like your turquoise linen shirt."

He might be a jerk, but he sure did know how to dress, she thought.

"This quilting is amazing. May I suggest?" The next thing Alice knew he was on his knees, re-pinning the unfinished hem of one of the kimonos.

Alice and Sophia exchanged confused glances. Sophia looked ravishing in a one shouldered green caftan. From the knees down, the silk looked as though it had been dipped in gold paint. The green brought out the shine in her long black hair and the healthy color in her cheeks. Alice immediately made a mental note to use gold accents on her costumes.

"Uh, Emelio, Sophia. Here are the ideas the committee has come up with." She gestured to the pages laid out on her glass-topped sales counter. Each page had smaller swatches of painted watercolor paper to show the color schemes. "They are all good, but..." She trailed off as they both stepped forward to examine the submissions.

"But they are not superfantastic," Sophia answered.

Emelio stood, his flush fading as he tucked his hands in his pockets. "Let's see what we have."

Hours later, Emelio, Sophia, and Alice walked over to Edna's Diner. Alice was so close to throttling Emelio, it was a wonder she hadn't been arrested. She'd finally suggested getting something to eat just as a distraction. Plus, she could use Edna's help to keep herself calm.

"As I said," Emelio continued, "your theme should be James Bond. Imagine the clothes."

Less than fifteen minutes ago, Sophia had suggested the long-lived movie franchise. Alice and Sophia exchanged glances. Alice was saddened to see the fatigue on Sophia's face. This was how he drained and diminished her friend. Why wouldn't she just ditch him and be done with it?

"Hello, darlings," Edna sang out as they entered the diner. Before Emelio could slide into the booth with the women, she said, "Emelio, my dear. Would you be willing to look over the week's menu? I would love to compare notes with such a well-known restauranteur."

He glanced at Sophia and Alice, his mouth pulling into a quick frown, his eyes tight and tired. "I don't think so. I am here to spend time with my Sophia."

Edna nodded. "Of course, of course. I'll just keep you ten minutes, then you can get back to pitching woo."

He sighed. Once he was through the pass-through and into the kitchen, Alice said, "How are you, sweetie?"

Sophia straightened the neckline of her caftan. "I enjoyed going over the themes. I think the upscale spy idea will be wonderful. It gives everyone a chance to wear beautiful clothes and be their most suave."

Alice didn't pursue her question, willing to follow where Sophia led. "We obviously will need a class on how to do fancy hair while you are here. All I can manage is a bun with lots of hair pins."

"We can do better than that." Sophia's grin wavered a bit when she looked over Alice's shoulder. "Ah, here comes Emelio." She closed her eyes, took a deep breath, and then plastered a smile on her face.

Over a delicious dinner of scallion pancakes and pork belly, Alice watched Emelio with a hawk's eye.

"This is quite good." He set down his fork, rubbed the back of his neck, and slid his eyes sideways.

What a liar, Alice thought. His pancake had no more than three bites out of it while she and Sophia were halfway through. Edna's food was delicious, but it was clear that Emelio wasn't as into food as a restauranteur should have been.

"What do you think, beloved, about adding more international cuisine to our restaurant?" he said, reaching out to take Sophia's hand. She avoided it by reaching for her glass of prosecco.

"*Our* restaurant?" Sophia demurely sipped her prosecco, her gaze lowered. Her tone held the tiniest hint of sarcasm. Emelio didn't notice, but Alice sure did. "I'm not sure, Emelio. How is the Roman market for the different cuisines?"

Alice hid her grin behind a bite of succulent pork belly. Sophia had his number, and she was going to be fine.

Alice pulled out her phone and sent a text to the group: *Looking good!*

Chapter Twenty-Two

*Love should make you more confident, more capable, and just
more. Walk away from love that makes you feel less.*

**How to Take Over the World: Affirmations for Glorious
Femmes**

The next morning, Alice stood in the archway that separated Henry's Hats from The Dream Factory. Love
overwhelmed her heart. Henry Higgins, her boyfriend, had
become a beacon and an inspiration to her. From the moment
they had first exchanged emails two years ago, she knew he was
someone special. Handsome, yes, but creative, interesting, and
an amazing listener. He had a way of looking into her eyes as
she spoke that let her know, more than any words could, that

she was important to him, that she was his person and that he
was happy about that.

She put her hands in her pockets and admired the hat he was
currently creating. A theater in St. Louis had ordered head-
wear for a production of *Alice in Wonderland*. For the Mad
Hatter, he had designed a top hat that looked like an enormous
spool of thread with a needle stuck between the fibers. Her
breath caught as she stared at his capable hands, moving swiftly
amongst the felt, glue, and leather. He was just so...competent,
and that was such a turn-on. Her soul demanded she finally
speak the words she'd been sitting on.

"Henry? Are you interruptible?" she asked.

"For you, of course," he answered, setting down his scissors.

Her nerves almost got the better of her, but she entered
the store, and got down on one knee next to Henry's work
chair. Maybe this wasn't the most romantic way to do this, but
she'd been thinking about it for ages, and it was just what she
wanted. His eyes were wide as she looked up and said, at last,
"Will you marry me?"

His jaw dropped. "What?"

Alice dragged in deep breath. "Will you marry me? Will you
combine businesses, finances, life insurance, and your life with
me?"

"Yes!" He laughed, leaning down to press a quick kiss to her lips. "Just one second." Henry reached over to his cash drawer, hit a button, and pulled out a velvet-covered box. "I was going to ask this weekend."

Her knees shook, but she was able to rise to her feet. "Really?"

"Really." He opened the box. The aquamarine in the yellow gold band sat between tiny, diamond-encrusted leaves, framing the main stone with shine and sparkle. "Aquamarine is supposed to bring feelings of inner peace and wash away stress."

"Oh," she gasped. Holding out her left hand, she trembled as he slid it on her left ring finger. The stones set off her dusky skin. "Oh, sweetheart." She couldn't believe that they'd both decided to ask at the same time. Talk about kismet.

"I was thinking we could get married in autumn, at The Thing. Where we first met."

"Yes, yes, a thousand times, yes." Tears gathered and poured down her cheeks.

Henry manfully wiped away his own tears. "I look forward to all the amazing things we will do throughout the years. Together. I love you, Alice."

Together. She really liked that word. "I love you, too, Henry."

While Emelio was off paying his traffic ticket, Blanche and Sophia studied the plans for the future farmer's market. Blanche pushed a piece of graph paper toward Sophia. "I've measured the new store. This is how I think all the goods should be displayed."

Sophia set down her glass of milk, leaned over her plate of Edna's Korean braised chicken, and picked up the map. "This looks really good. I think we should put your fresh goods in the window, though, instead of here in the back corner."

"Are you sure?" Blanche bit her lip. "That seems really egotistical."

Sophia raised an eyebrow. "Now, who told you that you should hide your light?"

Blanche shook her head and chuckled. "Okay. Now, why should I put my stuff in front?"

"Your vegetables are *the* draw for customers. Everyone wants your goods, and all the beautiful colors will lure them like nothing else. Get them in to buy the fresh produce, then everything else will entice them."

"Oh." Blanche blushed and touched the notch in her throat. "That makes so much sense. I know my eye is always caught when there is something pretty and colorful in the window."

"Exactly." Sophia reached for the pen in her purse to make some tweaks to Blanche's floorplan.

Just then, Henry and Alice burst through the door, enormous smiles on their faces. Everyone in the place turned to look, faces bright with curiosity.

"Everyone, we're getting married," Alice shouted.

"I'm the luckiest man in the world," Henry announced.

Edna lifted her arms in the air. "Woohoo! Congratulations. This calls for champagne. Hiram, bring out a bottle!"

Sal, the webmaster, Melvin, the doctor, and Howard, the sheriff, got out of their booth and hugged them hard, all three bursting with words of congratulations and pieces of advice.

Blanche and Sophia exchanged the glances of women who had had their hearts ripped out by love. "He'll be so good to her," Blanche said quietly. Together, they slid out from their chairs and joined in celebrating with the newly engaged couple.

Once she'd offered her congratulations, Sophia perched on a counter stool, watching the town slowly filter their way into Edna's Diner. Cassia and Katrina dashed over from the café. Raymond wandered in, patting Henry's shoulder and buying everyone glasses of champagne, forcing Edna to open a second bottle.

Marie shouted a greeting, her hands full of books on organizing a wedding. "They told me they'd be needed," she said, plopping them on the counter.

Laughter and joy filled the diner, bursting out the seems to swell through the town.

Had Emelio looked that happy to be with her? Had his face lit up with pride at her accomplishments? Or had he even looked at her like Henry looked at Alice, like she was precious and worth his time?

Not really, she realized. Oh, he'd been proud to have her on his arm when she was wearing something small and close-fitting. He'd been happy when she suggested things for his restaurant that helped boost his business and make him look good to the public. But he had never looked as radiant with her as Henry did with Alice. He might be a passionate lover, but he wasn't *in love* with her. She wasn't sure he could love anyone but himself.

She watched Alice meet Henry's gaze. Her body leaned into his, her smile was open and tender. Her shoulders were soft, not tight up toward her ears. There were no creases between her eyebrows. Everything about Alice said she felt safe, respected, cherished. Sophia remembered how the space between her shoulder blades always hurt after a date with Emelio.

It wasn't from laughing as she had thought at the time. It had been from keeping her emotional armor on, so his so-called teasing wouldn't hurt. It had been tension from bracing for the next jab, the next trauma.

Never again, she decided. She wanted a love that made her light up, not feel small. Her soul lightened, and she smiled at the happiness surrounding her. This was what she wanted. *This* is what she would have.

"More of this, please," she whispered as Edna handed her a glass of champagne. "Much more of this."

Chapter Twenty-Three

Manipulation is a broken skeleton key. You think it opens every-thing, yet it opens nothing.

How to Take Over the World: Affirmations for Glorious Femmes

E melio threw open the doors to the diner, not even giving an appreciative sniff for the familiar smell of yeast in an oven and the bubbling of something spicy. He'd been around too many cafes and bakeries to even enjoy the aromas of cinnamon and oranges and chocolate anymore. So here he was, in this uncultured, ugly place in the middle of nowhere, trying to swallow his distaste and win Sophia back. He just needed some time alone with her, except the townsfolk kept getting in the way. He would have suspected it was a plot, but he doubted anyone in town was that clever.

The only bright spot had been the moment looking over Alice's designs for the play. He hadn't expected to see that high level of tailoring in this small space.

The crowd around him in this insignificant diner cheered as Alice and Henry burbled about their future together. What did he care what two small-town nobodies did with their lives? They were stuck here in this depressing village with no future, no chance at fame or fortune. And people cheered for this?

Sophia glanced over at him. He schooled his face into a pleasant expression, as if he were just as thrilled for the couple. It wouldn't do for her to see his disgust at how these people were making a foolish spectacle of themselves. He could, though, use the so-called romance of the moment to pressure Sophia into doing what he wanted. She was so easily manipulated by sentiment. It was how he'd kept her distracted from seeing who he really was.

He quickly crossed the linoleum floor and slid into the booth across from her. He captured her hand and caressed her fingers with slow strokes, widening his eyes slightly to make himself appear warm and sincere. "Sophia. Cara mia. I leave this afternoon. Will you come home to me when you are done here?"

Chapter Twenty-Four

It's not saying good-bye to someone. It's saying hello to yourself.
How to Take Over the World: Affirmations for Glorious Femmes

Sophia inhaled, her breath sticking in her lungs. Her stomach lurched and her palms felt both cold and sweaty at the same time. Here it was, the answer to the question that had driven her to Gold Coast. He *did* want her. He had traveled thousands of miles all the way from Rome, had rented a very expensive car, and had been patient while the town interrupted them over and over. All to win her back.

But now she had a new question: Did *she* want him back?

She'd seen who he was. What was the famous saying? When someone shows you who they are, believe them? Not once in this time together had he asked what she wanted in life, what she was doing with her time here in Gold Coast. He hadn't even been happy about Cheryl's and Pamela's makeovers. The whole time, he'd sat outside and stared at his phone while the rest of the town congratulated the girls on their new looks and Sophia on her creative talent. He wouldn't even do the basics of a healthy relationship. How could he possibly make for a good partner in life?

Saying yes to him would be the end of her world. The very thought made her sick. She would tell him the truth.

Why did she feel dread pooling low in her stomach at the idea of saying what she needed?

Maybe because she didn't like upsetting people.

Maybe because she knew he would react very badly.

She must have taken too long, or perhaps he saw her hesitation. His hands and features stiffened and something shifted in his gaze. For just a moment there was an ugliness to him she'd never seen before. No, that was a lie. She'd seen it before when he'd confronted her outside her family's bakery after he'd ended their relationship. He'd been ugly like this then and she'd been afraid, truly afraid. It had been Cassie who'd stepped in and stood up for her.

That told her everything she needed to know.

But before she could say a word, he schooled his features and gave her a weak smile and wide eyes. Normally she would have fallen for it, but she felt nothing. She knew without a doubt that smile wasn't real. Emelio had played his grand gesture, but she was done with him.

She slid her hand from beneath his, stiffening her spine and bracing for what she knew was to come. Her mouth was dry and sticky, but her stomach had settled. She knew beyond a shadow of a doubt she was making the right choice. She didn't need him to make her life exciting and vibrant. She was exciting and vibrant all on her own.

She looked him straight in the eyes. "I'm sorry. We want different things. I won't be coming back to you ever."

Chapter Twenty-Five

Self-care rituals give you the courage to ride through the storm.

How to Take Over the World: Affirmations for Glorious

Femmes

Emelio's eyes glittered with malice. The muscles in his jaw flexed. "Someday, you'll see everything you passed up and you'll want me back," he hissed, his voice like poison. "And I'll say no. Because you aren't good enough. You never were."

Sophia opened her mouth to defend herself, but he kept going, his low voice somehow even nastier and meaner than if he'd shouted.

"You arrogant witch." Hot, ugly color suffused his face, turning it florid. "You think that you are better than me?

Think that you can make it without me and my friends pushing your business?" He pushed his finger in her face as he rose from the booth. "All you'll ever be is used and dumped because you will never amount to anything. No one will ever want you. You'll be a pathetic hairdresser with chapped hands all your life. I put you on the map and I can take you off it."

With that, he stalked out of Edna's Diner, rudely shoving aside the townsfolk as he went. They ignored him, focused as they were on the party.

Sophia stood there, shuddering at his hateful words as the rest of the town celebrated Alice and Henry's love. She knew that Emelio held people in contempt—part of her had always known it—but she hadn't known that she was one of those people or that his contempt for her was so great. Why would he even bother to ask her to go with him if he detested her that much?

Because he isn't the one who made you, child. You made him and he hates you for it. She could swear she heard her grandmother's voice whisper in her ear. Impossible, of course, but it did make it sting a little less.

Numb, she watched him through the big windows as he shoved his duffle in the yellow Lamborghini, and climbed in.

He slammed the door and roared off, leaving black tire marks on the pavement.

Howard's head turned at the aggressive noise. Sophia saw him track Emelio as he left town, driving over the railroad tracks and onto the big highway. Howard spoke into the radio on his shoulder. Probably telling his deputies to keep an eye out. Wise. Even in the best of times, Emelio was not a careful driver.

After he was done speaking, Howard glanced at her and frowned in concern. "What happened?"

Sophia stared at Howard, her mouth still open in shock. "I... He..." She breathed for a second, letting her wild emotions settle into place. "I said no."

"And he didn't like that." Howard placed a hand on her shoulder. It was surprisingly comforting. "What did he say to you?"

Howard's rose and spice cologne snuck out from under his shirt sleeve. The wafting scent teased her, set up a memory of helping the women in the town. It made her feel suddenly stronger, surer of herself. Her grandmother's voice—real or imagined—was right. Emelio hadn't made her. He hadn't done anything. She had made herself. She and the people of this town. His anger had no power over her.

She gave a tiny laugh. "Bullshit. He said a lot of bullshit that I know isn't true."

Howard smiled. "I don't doubt that. And you know what they say you ought to do with a pile of manure."

She was a city girl. She had no idea, so she shrugged. "Toss it out?"

"No, my dear," he said with a boyish grin. "Use it. Manure makes some of the best fertilizer. What do you think Raymond uses on those roses of his?" Then with a chuckle, he turned and rejoined the revelers.

Sophia stood for a moment, eyeing him thoughtfully. *Use it.* How did one use angry, hateful words as fertilizer?

A slow smile spread across her face. Fertilizer was a sort of fuel, wasn't it? A fuel to increase the growth of plants and make them lush and healthy. She would use Emelio's bullshit to fuel her inner fire to plant her ideas and make them grow just as lush and healthy. He thought she couldn't do anything on her own? That he was the man behind the woman? That he *made* her? That her job was insignificant? Well, he wasn't in Gold Coast anymore and he hadn't lifted a finger to help her or anyone else while he was here. He'd scoffed at the idea of the co-op. In fact, he'd sneered at this whole town.

She would show everyone that Gold Coast was a wonderful, amazing place and the women in this town had so much to offer. And it would all begin with the co-op. She couldn't wait to get started!

But for now, there was an engagement to celebrate. She lifted her glass and joined in the fun.

The morning after Henry and Alice got engaged, Sophia knocked on Blanche's door. Her friend appeared, looking a bit flushed, her hair up in a neat braid. Sophia smiled to herself. At last, Blanche was no longer hiding herself away.

"Oh, Sophia!" Blanche said, swinging open the creaky old screen door. "You don't have to knock. Just come on in."

"Am I interrupting something?"

"Not at all." Blanche led the way into the kitchen. "I'm trying a new recipe for anti-aging skin cream. I'm making my own rosehip oil. According to my research, it brightens the skin and aids elasticity and collagen production. Can you imagine all that from something most people throw away?"

Sophia smiled. She did know, of course, but she was delighted to see the excitement on her friend's face at discovering something so wonderful. "That's amazing, Blanche. Nature offers us so many astounding things, don't you think?"

"For sure!" Blanche laughed in delight. "Just wait until the violets bloom again. I'm going to make a moisturizer for oily skin. Maybe even some tea!"

The kitchen smelled heavenly, fresh and herbal. Something simmered away in a double boiler on the large, farmhouse stove, and various oils and other ingredients were lined up in front of an ancient mustard-yellow blender.

"Moisturizer would be a wonderful addition to the store," Sophia said.

Blanche beamed. "That's what I thought."

"Do you know how you want to package it?"

"Honestly, I hadn't thought about it," Blanche admitted. "For right now I was just going to put it in old jam jars, but I suppose it should be something fancy for the store."

"Not necessarily," Sophia said. "I have an idea. May I show you?"

"Of course!"

Sophia pulled her laptop out of her bag and placed it on the kitchen table. She flipped it open and tapped a few keys. "How about fancy labels? And a photo shoot?"

Blanche's eyes lit up. "Tell me more."

Chapter Twenty-Six

Celebrate every step you take to fulfill your dreams.

How to Take Over the World: Affirmations for Glorious Femmes

Sal finished nailing the Gold Coast Farmer's Market sign to the front of the clean and fully stocked store right above the door. He shimmied down the ladder and waved to Blanche and Sophia. "All yours, ladies," he called out as he folded and carried it away.

Blanche and Sophia stood back to admire it and the big sign in the window that read, "Grand Opening All Week!!"

"Oh, Sophia," Blanche breathed, tucking a stray lock of hair behind her ear. Sophia had helped her style it this morning for the grand opening. "It looks amazing."

Alice nodded. "It really does." She stood next to Blanche; her hand entwined with Henry's. "Even better than I imagined it would. When you first brought it up, I thought it would be rustic and rough and ready, like a farm stand, but this is gorgeous."

They'd spent the last couple of weeks since Emelio left working from dawn until dusk to get the shop ready. They'd cleaned and sanded and painted every inch of the place, installed shelves and display tables, and generally gave the place a TV-worthy makeover. And now they were finally ready to open. Sophia felt so proud—of herself and her friends—that she didn't know whether to burst into tears or dance in the street.

"Let's get ready," Sophia said, leading them into the shop. "It's almost time."

Inside, Leilani Jones, wearing her long black hair up in a twisted, swoopy bun, put the last of the cheeses from her farm away in the refrigerator. She'd agreed to supply chevre from her goats and a simple farm-style cheese from her cows. If things went well, she'd agreed to try her hand at other types of cheese.

Closing the fridge door, she put her hands on her hips and smiled. "Everything looks delicious."

Sophia beamed. Green paper containers of plump red raspberries and strawberries filled the shelving in front of the windows. By the front door, individual buckets of water held different aromatic bouquets. One bucket held masses of lavender, another, giant branches of rosemary, and the rest held varieties of roses, daisies, and sunflowers.

Matching brown baskets held green beans, white papery bulbs of garlic, huge green heads of leafy lettuces, basil, and parsley. Against the back wall, cobalt blue bottles held Blanche's various hydrosols, colognes, linen sprays, and laundry supplies. Next to them, Sophia's hair and skin care potions in their vintage perfume bottles enticed the eye. And, of course, there were the vintage jam jars filled with Blanche's special anti-aging cream, topped with art nouveau labels. Sophia and Marie had taken some time in the rose garden to shoot promotional images of Cheryl, Pamela, Blanche, and Joan for the different formulas. They'd each sported a hat by Henry and an outfit made by Alice to give the impression of a vintage vibe.

Owen Pux and Edna admired the shining store. "Girls," Owen said, "you all have an excellent eye. This packaging looks amazing."

Edna beamed at the gorgeous fruit display. "I love it," she declared. "It's like having a little restaurant row right here in Gold Coast." She adjusted a cute wooden sign by the cash register that read, *"Why have plain when you can have fancy?"*

Sophia beamed. This was what she'd imagined when she first came to Gold Coast and saw the shop. Working together to create something beautiful and useful. To lift the spirits both of those in the co-op and those who would become their customers. To show the world that Gold Coast held not only delightful goods but also wonderfully creative people.

"Are you ready?" Cassie asked, leaning closer. She'd come in early to finish stocking the shelves.

Sophia nodded. "Yes." Then louder, "Turn the sign, Blanche."

With a beaming smile, Blanche flipped the "Closed" sign over to "Open."

"Ladies and gentlemen," Sophia said, "we're open for business."

A cheer echoed up and down the street.

And in an upstairs window overlooking the new shop, Betsy and Lucia gave each other a high-five.

Epilogue

J oan Marks placed a bouquet of daisies on the scrubbed
clean kitchen table in her house. She was still pinching
pennies, but she had remembered what Alice Kennedy had
said.

"We need bread *and* roses," she'd whispered to Joan as they
stood in the doorway of the new Farmer's Market.

It was so true, Joan decided. Practical was fine and good, but
a woman needed to feed her soul. Besides, she was feeling a little
flush.

When they were at the grand opening, Leilani had talked to
her about buying some of the acreage currently going fallow
on the Marks' family farm. Eli had been a bully and a jerk, but
he had been the one with the passion for farming. She'd kept

the books and did the food, but darn it, she was flat tired out of the heavy labor. She had no interest in continuing the farming tradition. Let someone with a passion for it do it.

If Joan sold off that property, she'd have enough money to restore the house and the shed and set up that bed and breakfast she'd thought about for years. That was *her* passion. She could well imagine serving her guests fresh scones from the bakery along with her own homemade jams. Placing bouquets of flowers in their rooms and filling the bathrooms with Blanche and Sophia's body care products.

"Hello? Joan?" Sophia's lilting accent floated through the front door.

"Oh, come on in, dear." Joan smiled. How wonderful it was to have a glamorous, intelligent friend, she thought. One with an eye for design and beauty. One who didn't look down her nose at an old farming woman.

Not old, she reminded herself. *You're in your goddess years.*

"Oh, what lovely flowers," Sophia crooned, touching the petals of the cheery bouquet in the center of the table. Joan had made it herself and Sophia's praise filled her with pride at her accomplishment.

After lemonade and radishes with butter, Joan took Sophia around the house. She explained her plans for the place and how she might run her business.

"I see what you mean," the Italian woman said. "This could be a very peaceful place. I could see it being very popular with writers and artists, especially if you get Blanche to plant a pretty garden. Painters love gardens. You could eventually remodel the old barn into a meeting space for writer and artist retreats. It could double as a banquet hall for weddings and parties."

Joan's mouth dropped. The best she had thought would be for honeymooners on a budget. Why else would anyone want to come to this corner of nowhere? "Artists?" she gulped. "Writers?"

"Silence, a view, and someone else doing the cooking? Yes, it would be perfect for that clientele." Sophia spun around the bare formal dining room. Joan had cleaned out all of Eli's dirty tractor parts and washed the walls.

"How do you think this should look?" she asked Sophia.

"I am not an interior designer," Sophia demurred. "Let us look at what you like and go from there." She pointed at a stack of library books on the card table in the corner. "I see you have talked to Marie."

Joan laughed. "She made sure I was stocked up with books. I had no idea we had books on design at the library." Marie was darn good at her job, for sure. It was as if the books jumped off the shelves and into her arms, each one perfect for the patron it was meant for.

"Point out the things you like." Sophia pulled up a chair, swung her long hair over one shoulder and flipped open a book on Morocco. "We will just put a bookmark on pages you feel drawn to and we will go from there."

Three hours later, Joan's sides hurt from all the laughter. They had slips of colored paper sticking out of every book except for the one on the 'farmhouse' aesthetic. "I've lived my whole life in farmhouses," she said. "I want something a little more ...." She waved her hands around.

"Bohemian?" Sophia supplied. "Colorful? Whimsical?"

"Yes. Bohemian but comfortable." She pointed to a chair that looked like a grinning coconut. "This is cool, but I don't think anyone would want to put their feet up or settle in for hours."

Sophia beamed. "My lovely Joan. You have a better eye than you think."

After that, they stood up and hugged. "In two days, I leave Gold Coast a much happier person than when I arrived,"

Sophia said. "Thank you, Joan, for letting me play with you. Now, you will remember to spoil yourself, yes?"

"Yes." Joan promised. "I wish you didn't have to go back to Italy."

Sophia smiled gently. "I feel like I belong to two worlds now: Rome and Gold Coast. I can't wait to come back. And the next time I visit, I will be able to stay with you and not share lovely Cassia's little bed." She kissed Joan's cheeks. "You will be a mad success, I know it."

As Sophia drove away toward town in Eli's beat-up old truck which she'd borrowed from Cassie, Joan's heart felt warm and happy. She'd not been safe, let alone happy, for so long. She was going to grab this emotion with both hands and never let go.

After all, she had dreams now.

The end

Authors' Note

Thank you so much for reading Sophia's book! We both enjoy choosing fancy over plain and I hope this story inspires you to lift yourself in lush, wonderful ways.

Independent authors love reviews. They are the yummies that keep us writing. Let us know what you like and what you want to see more of. □

Our email addresses are:

lindamercuryromance@gmail.com

sheamacleodauthor@gmail.com

Also by Linda Mercury

Fiction

The Blood Wings Trilogy

Dracula's Secret

Dracula's Desires

Dracula Unleashed

Auntie Vamp series

Vamping It Up

Keeping It Up

Stand Alones

Curse of the Spider Woman

Linda Mercury's Naughty Notes

Predator and Prey

The Dream Factory series

(co-authored with Shéa Macleod)

The Dream Factory

The Café of Hopes and Dream

A Dream of Words

Dream of Scent

Non-Fiction

Affirmations for Women in Business

Start Your Life Now: Affirmations for Women

Arousal to Zipper: Writing the Best Sex of Your Life

Handcuffs Teach Trust: Writing the Best BDSM of Your Life

Rejections, Bad Reviews, and Mean People: Illigitimi non Carborundum

Immediate and lasting relief from the nasty things people can say.

The Little Sexy Workbook: How to talk about your sex life in a fun and productive way.

Also by Shéa MacLeod

Lady Rample Sits In

Lady Rample and the Ghost of Christmas Past

Lady Rample and Cupid's Kiss

Lady Rample and the Mysterious Mr. Singh

Lady Rample and the Haunted Manor

Lady Rample and the Parisian Affair

Lady Rample and the Yuletide Caper

Lady Rample and the Mystery at the Museum

Lady Rample and the Lady in the Lake

Sugar Martin Vintage Cozy Mysteries

A Death in Devon

A Grave Gala

A Christmas Caper

A Riviera Rendezvous

Viola Roberts Cozy Mysteries

The Corpse in the Cabana

The Stiff in the Study

The Poison in the Pudding

The Body in the Bathtub

The Venom in the Valentine

The Remains in the Rectory

The Death in the Drink

The Victim in the Vineyard

The Ghost in the Graveyard

The Larceny in the Luau

Deepwood Witches Mysteries

Potions, Poisons, and Peril

Wisteria, Witchery, and Woe

Moonlight, Magic, and Murder

Dreams, Divination, and Danger

Alchemy, Arsenic, and Alibis

Crystals, Cauldrons, and Crime

Edwina Gale, Paranormal Investigator

Day of the Were-Jackal

Season of the Witch

Lifestyles of the Witch and Ageless

In Charm's Way

Witchmas Spirits

Battle of the Hexes

If the Broom Fits

RomComs

Notting Hill Diaries

The Art of Kissing Frogs

To Kiss a Prince

Kiss Me, Chloe

Kiss Me, Stupid

Kissing Mr. Darcy